Hunting Charlie Wilson

Book II of the Galhadrian Trilogy

Jan-Andrew Henderson

Black Hart Entertainment

Edinburgh. Scotland

First published Oxford University Press, Oxford 2005
Published by Black Hart, Edinburgh 2020
Black Hart Entertainment.
32 Glencoul Ave, Dalgetty Bay, Fife KY11 9XL.

Cover by Panagiotis Lampridis (BookDesignStars)
Book Layout © 2017 BookDesignTemplates.com

Hunting Charlie Wilson.
978-1-64826-885-4
978-1-64826-921-9 eBook

Some folklorists believe that King Arthur once lived and fought in Scotland... Possibly he was a Celtic Cavalry leader with a swift-moving force

Raymond Lamont-Brown. *Scottish Folklore.*

For Harper

Chapters

Part 1

The Chase Begins

I've had that recurring dream since I was a child, and a lot of people have different versions of that same dream, where you're running away from something, and it's going kind of slowly, but it's catching up with you, and it will not stop, and you cannot get away from it.

Paul W. S. Anderson

Gary MacMillan

Something was hunting Charlie Wilson.

It was lunch hour and he was sitting alone in the shadow of the science building, a secluded port-a-cabin near the edge of the school grounds. The structure was perched on the brink of a steep, scrub-covered hill and was Charlie's favourite spot. Just below the crest of the slope, he could look right across the town of Fenton to the patchwork of farmlands beyond. And nobody could see him.

Or so he thought.

At the foot of the hill, under a tangled thicket, hate-filled eyes glared up at the boy. Drooling black lips stretched back over needle-sharp teeth and the creature stalking Charlie began to inch uphill, gently worming through the stalks of bushes, so the green tops wouldn't move and alert its prey.

Charlie reached into his schoolbag and pulled out a red notebook with his name and address written on the front. His English teacher had given the class a writing assignment - *What I Did on My Holiday* - and he was having real problems with it. Not because he thought it was a boring topic.

Quite the opposite, in fact.

He opened the notebook and looked at what he'd written so far.

MY HOLIDAY
by Charlie Wilson

I spent last summer at the Edinburgh Festival in Scotland. My parents were performing in a show. Edinburgh had lots of old buildings and a big castle in the middle of the town. I met a girl called Lilly who was one of the Little People or Galhadrians, as they call themselves. She turned out to be hundreds of years old.

I discovered some hidden tunnels under the city and found an old diary there. It belonged to a pickpocket called Peazle, who lived in the 19th century. Long ago, he and his friends, Duncan and Shadowjack Henry, found monsters called the Gorrodin Rath trapped in the tunnels. They managed to destroy them, but they missed the leader, Mordred. Lilly was staying around to make sure Mordred never got out. I quite liked Lilly.

Anyway, I found King Arthur's sword, Excalibur, and killed Mordred with it.

That was my summer holiday.

"Can't see that I'll get A+ for this," he muttered to himself, tearing out the page and crumpling it into a ball. The really annoying thing was, the story was completely true, but Charlie knew nobody would believe it.

Besides, he had promised Lilly that he would keep the existence of Galhadrians a secret.

"I'll just have to make something boring up instead," he sighed.

The creature was now halfway up the slope, belly low to the ground and claws digging into the dirt, as it pulled its body through the foliage. It uttered an impatient gargling growl and saliva spilled over its glistening jaws onto the torn earth.

Charlie was about to start writing again when he heard a rasping voice floating over the crest of the hill.

"What you looking at, eh? You looking at me?"

The boy recognised it immediately and groaned to himself. The voice belonged to Gary Macmillan.

Gary Macmillan was the school bully, a pasty-faced youth with bad teeth and oily hair. He was also broader and stronger than most boys his age and stood at least a head taller than the others in his class. Charlie scrambled up the incline and peered over the top. Macmillan had a smaller boy pinned against the wall of the building. Behind him stood the bully's two sidekicks - Watson and Brogan - sniggering behind their leader, like hyenas waiting for scraps.

"I seen the way you were looking at me," Macmillan sneered. "Now I'm going to have you."

Gary Macmillan's victim kept his eyes down, afraid to anger his attacker further. His lip was trembling as he tried his best not to cry.

The old Charlie Wilson would have ducked quietly down again rather than interfere. After all, Macmillan was twenty pounds heavier than he was and had two thugs helping him. But the summer adventure had changed him. He was no longer the kind of boy to walk away from something so wrong.

The creature was hauling itself through the last few yards of thinning undergrowth when Charlie put his notebook back into his schoolbag and stood up. It flattened itself to the ground with an enraged hiss, as the boy turned and walked away.

The bullies had their back to Charlie and didn't notice he was there until, heart pounding, he stepped between Brogan and Watson and tapped Gary Macmillan on the shoulder. As the youth looked round in surprise, Charlie hit him as hard as he could, right between the eyes. The bully staggered backwards several feet before landing flat on his back. Seeing his chance, Macmillan's victim turned and fled.

Brogan and Watson stared at the newcomer in astonishment. Nobody had ever dared pick a fight with Gary Macmillan. Charlie turned on them.

"What you looking at, eh?" he leered.

Macmillan staggered to his feet, his expression of pain turning instantly to one of rage. Before he could advance, there came a roar from behind the group.

"Wilson! What do you think you're doing?" A large, hairy hand landed on Charlie's shoulder, spinning him round. He found himself looking at the bearded face of Mr Swift, the school's Physical Education teacher.

"I came round the corner just in time to see you hit that lad," Mr Swift fumed. "I trust you have a good explanation for your conduct?"

Charlie shrugged.

"Ehm… I didn't know you were about to come round the corner?"

Mr Swift turned bright red.

The boy looked over his shoulder as the PE teacher hauled him off to the headmaster's office. Gary Macmillan was glaring after them, face still contorted in anger.

I'll get you for this, the bully mouthed.

Hidden by bushes, the creature bit into Charlie's forgotten schoolbag with a fury Macmillan could never match and silently tore it apart.

The Whistle and the Bear

That night, Charlie's father came to his room. He sat on the bed and looked awkwardly around, picking up half-finished plastic models his son had been working on and putting them down again. Finally, he exhaled loudly, as if he had been holding his breath.

"I got a phone call from the principal at your school today. He said you hit a boy."

Having run out of models to study, Charlie's father began to scan the posters of pop stars on the wall. He wondered how some of them got their hair to stick up like that.

"Did you punch someone called Gary Macmillan?" he asked at last.

"Yes, I did."

"Care to tell me why?"

"Because he's a bully," Charlie said defiantly. "He picks on smaller kids and they're too scared to tell anyone about it." Despite his bravado, the boy's voice began to quiver.

"Now he and his friends are going to be after me, because I tried to help. I'm scared, dad."

"Why on earth did you get involved?"

Charlie had been thinking about this all day and could only come up with one answer. After all, he had fought another monster for the very same reason.

"It was the right thing to do," he said simply.

Charlie's father looked taken aback. He glanced up at the ceiling, which he always did when he was lost for something to say. Then he reached out and gently touched the boy's face.

"For what it's worth, son, you've made me very proud."

He stood up and put his hands in his pockets. Charlie remained sitting on the bed and both looked at each other. Charlie's father walked to the bedroom door and opened it, then paused, rubbing his chin thoughtfully.

"You know Charlie; there are two great virtues a man can have. One is knowing what is right. The other is doing what is right. Today you showed that you have both."

"Yeah," the boy scowled. "I'm going to get a total pasting for it, too."

"Unfortunately, virtue often has to be its own reward," his father admitted before he left.

"Is that supposed to cheer me up?" Charlie muttered to the closing door.

An hour later, there was a gentle tap and his mum slipped quietly into the room. The boy looked up from his book and raised an eyebrow. His mother and father were good to their son, but seemed to prefer each other's company. For both to visit in one night was an unusual occurrence. Charlie's mother plonked herself onto the bed in the same place where her husband had sat not long before.

"Your dad and I have had a talk," she said. "He thinks we've been very selfish, dragging you from place to place, just so we can do the work we want. You never get a chance to settle down."

Charlie couldn't argue with that. His parents were professional acrobats and moved around the country, chasing the small number of jobs open to their rather unusual profession. The boy had changed schools several times in his few short years and it had been hard for him to make any real friends.

"That's going to change," his mother continued decisively. "You don't like Fenton much anyway, do you?"

"Not really."

"Then we'll move one last time." Charlie's mother caught the look of resignation on her son's face and raised her hand. "But this *is* the last time, I promise. We've decided to go to Birmingham and we're staying put when we get there."

"Really?" Charlie couldn't keep a note of suspicion out of his voice.

"Really. Your father has decided to get a steady job." She smiled at her son's astonishment and ruffled his hair. "To be honest, he never liked wearing those spangled acrobat's tights much. He just did it to please me."

She lowered her voice to a whisper.

"He'd probably rather work in a bank."

"Are we going to go soon?" Charlie asked, thinking of Gary Macmillan.

"Why wait? Your father is going to look for work tomorrow and I'll sort out somewhere for us to live. We can stay with my friend Shirley in Birmingham for the next few days while we get things finalised." His mother gave a knowing wink. "So you don't have to worry about this bully anymore."

Charlie blinked rapidly. His parents weren't big on planning ahead but this was a snap decision, even by their standards.

"This is a bit sudden,"

"Remember what your dad is always telling you?" his mother said. "That hesitation is an acrobat's worst enemy? There's no point in saying something unless you're willing to act on it."

"What will *you* do in the city?" the boy asked tentatively.

"I was thinking of becoming a nightclub singer." Charlie's mum pushed her hair over her face and struck a provocative pose. "I look too good in spangles to give it up."

The boy grinned, despite himself. He knew his mother could never do anything normal. She let her hair drop back down and looked solemnly at him.

"Joking aside, your father is making a great sacrifice for you," she said quietly. "You know why?"

Charlie shook his head.

"Because he's not afraid to do the right thing either. And because you're worth it."

As she spoke, she reached round the back of her neck and unfastened the silver chain she always wore. On the end dangled a small, exquisitely carved metallic bear.

"I notice you've taken to wearing a little whistle around your neck," she said. "I don't even know who you got it from."

Charlie stayed silent. The whistle had been a parting gift from Lilly, the Galhadrian who guarded Edinburgh's tunnels. But he couldn't exactly tell his mother that.

She gently reached out and fastened the chain around the boy's neck. The bear clinked against the whistle with a musical ring.

"I got this from *my* mother." She tapped the glittering amulet. "It's the most precious thing I own in the whole world."

"I can't take this." Charlie tried to unfasten the clasp. "Not if it means so much to you."

"No, it's yours now. To show how much I love you."

Charlie's eyes filled with tears. His parents had never acted like this before. He gave the bear a grateful squeeze and tucked it into his pyjama top.

"I'll never take it off," he said.

"You'd better not. It's very lucky and the most precious thing I own, so you must take care of it."

Charlie's mum cleared her throat loudly and gave his hand a brief pat, as if she had used up all her emotions for one night. Then she kissed him quickly on the cheek and left.

"If this keeps up, I'll be wearing more jewellery than a New York rapper," the boy mumbled. But he was secretly happy, for each token was proof someone cared for him.

He lay awake for a long time, staring at the ceiling and smiling to himself, all thoughts of Gary Macmillan banished from his mind. He was too excited to sleep so, eventually, he got out of bed and went to the window. Charlie's parents didn't have a lot of money and the street where they lived was rather run down, dimly lit and lined with small uniform gardens. Their own small plot was overrun with weeds ringed by untidy bushes. Charlie's parents weren't big on gardening. The boy stretched, yawned, and looked down into the undergrowth.

A pair of yellow eyes stared up at him from a tangle of shrubs.

The boy's heart leapt and he felt the hairs rise on his neck. He let out a shuddering breath and, instinctively, grasped the chains around his neck.

"It's a cat," he whispered to himself. "Of course. Just a cat."

But he knew it was far too big to be a cat. And as his eyes adjusted to the dusky light, he could now make out a large, thick body. Then the creature slid sideways and vanished into the darkness below the garden wall. Seconds later, the front gate swung violently open, slammed shut, and he had a brief glimpse of something bobbing through the shadows and down the street.

Charlie scanned the rest of the road but dirty orbs of the streetlights revealed nothing out of the ordinary. Finally, he went back to bed.

"It must have been a dog, then," he frowned. "A big dog. Or maybe a badger."

He clutched the bear and whistle and closed his eyes tightly. He still couldn't sleep - but now he had a different reason.

The Wilsons' front gate had a strong spring and a child-proof latch that clicked shut automatically.

Whatever let itself out of the garden had to have hands.

In the Whale Room

The man in the green tunic sat on a polished stairway in a great silver chamber, his head resting wearily in his hands. He was tall and thin with long dark hair and the goose feathers threaded through the turned-down tops of his leather boots marked him out as a great wizard.

There was a hesitant tap on the massive oak door at the other end of the chamber and the sorcerer quickly straightened his back. He nodded towards the door, which swung silently open. A small boy stood in the brightly lit entrance, like Jonah peering into the glistering jaws of a mighty whale.

The high vaulted chamber was as lofty and ornate as any Cathedral and the giant silver arches that soared to the roof resembled the ribs of some massive leviathan, so the chamber was known as the Whale Room.

The boy squared his shoulders and marched over to the wizard on the staircase. The newcomer was small and wiry, wearing a brightly patterned waistcoat and bowler hat. In his hand, he carried a large metal briefcase that looked strangely at odds with his eccentric clothes.

"I ought to have picked up a pair of sunglasses on my trip," he said, squinting around the dazzling interior.

The sorcerer stood up and descended the stairs to meet him.

"Welcome back to Galhadria, Master Peazle," he said, lifting his hand in greeting.

"Thank you, Jack Thane."

The wizard indicated for Peazle to sit. There was no furniture in the Whale Room, so the child perched on the bottom step with the briefcase on his knee, like some miniature insurance salesman in fancy dress. Though they shone like polished glass, the steps were not slippery and the chamber, despite its vast size, wasn't cold.

"Well then, Peazle." Jack Thane tilted his head inquisitively to one side. "What have you brought from the world of men, this time?"

The boy set the case on the mirrored floor and popped the latches. He opened the lid and stood up again. In each hand, he held a gun with a short, thick barrel.

"These are called BK-8000 semi-automatic pistols," he replied, awe and fear equally evident in his voice. "Human weapons. Absolutely no recoil. Each can fire a single shot or a three-bullets-per-second burst with ten settings in between and they have a range of almost quarter of a mile. This is the weapon of choice if you want to absolutely, positively kill every single…. eh… person in the room."

"Your skills as a thief have not diminished, I'm glad to say," the wizard nodded. "Did you spirit these away from the tent of some great warrior?"

"Actually, I ordered it on the internet." Peazle scowled, unsure whether the wizard was joking or not. "I'm not a pickpocket anymore, Master Thane. I'm more of a… scholar."

Jack Thane grunted.

"Show me," he said. "Show me this semi-atomic plimsol."

"Show you?" The boy looked around the spotless hall. "In here? You sure?"

The wizard nodded.

"All right." Taking a deep breath, the boy tightened his finger on the trigger and swept one of the guns in an arc above his head. The weapon made a rapid put-putting rasp, no louder than air being let out of a balloon. Forty feet up, gouts of silver erupted from the walls of the Whale Room and danced and spun in the air. The gun was suddenly silent again, and Jack Thane and Peazle watched as metal shards dropped to the floor with a musical clatter. The boy looked embarrassed, as if he'd broken some elderly aunt's favourite vase. He blew a pale wisp of smoke from the pistol's barrel.

"It's almost like magic," he said, by way of an excuse.

"Almost." Thane agreed, waving his arm in a casual way. The boy jumped as if he had received an electric shock and looked down at his hands. He gave a short gasp. The gun, like the rest of the room, was now solid silver. The case, ammunition and spent cartridges around his feet were silver too, a deadly fortune scattered across the floor.

"Now, *that's* magic," The Galhadrian sniffed.

"If you don't mind, I'd like to go to the great library and return to my studies." Peazle put the gun back in its case and snapped the lid shut. He looked as if he was about to say something else, then thought better of it. But nothing escaped the attention of Jack Thane.

"Speak your mind, friend," he snapped brusquely. "This place has too many secrets already."

Peazle stood up, clutching the case to his chest like a shield.

"Science is mankind's magic," he said defiantly. "You must realise that, someday, men will also be able to turn lead into silver. And more than that, I fear."

The wizard suddenly looked tired. He sat slowly down on the step again, a movement that put his eyes level with those of the standing boy. So he closed them.

"Peazle... I need you to go back to the world of mankind, right away," he said gravely. "There has been a rather unfortunate... development there."

Jack Thane opened his pale green eyes again and fixed them on his little companion.

"You mean something terrible has happened." The pickpocket scowled.

"You could put it like that." The wizard considered the best way to elaborate and finally decided just to start at the beginning. He took a deep breath and began.

"Long ago, a creature of great evil walked the land of men. Her name was Morgana. Like her son Mordred, she was leader of the monsters known as the Gorrodin Rath."

He saw fear ignite in the pickpocket's eyes. Peazle had fought the Gorrodin Rath when he lived on earth. He still had nightmares about it

"She vanished during a great battle with a knight called Arthur and I thought her dead. I believe now I was wrong."

Thane's lips twitched. He didn't like being wrong.

"I think she has returned."

"What? Where?" Peazle looked around to make sure that Morgana wasn't lurking in a corner.

"I don't know that either," Jack Thane admitted bitterly. "My fellow wizards still doubt she is alive but I am sure. And dark creatures have been seen on earth…."

"What has all this got to do with me?"

"I assume Morgana has sent her foul minions after a certain human child. I want you to rescue him."

"In that case, you should send someone bigger. Like yourself, for instance."

Jack Thane shook his head in irritation.

"Magical creatures do not fight each other, Peazle, you know that."

"I know, I know," the boy sighed. "And you Galhadrians don't interfere in the lives of men." He stole a sideways glance at the figure in green. "So you want to send a lowly human."

The wizard waved his hand again and the silver wall behind Peazle began to glow softly. The pickpocket turned in time to see a faint picture forming. It seemed to be a boy lying on a bed. Peazle couldn't be sure, for the details were unclear, as if he were looking through a frosted window.

"When you first came to my land," Thane said. "How long ago was it?"

"You took me to Galhadria nearly 200 years ago." Peazle sounded annoyed the sorcerer didn't remember. "And, yes, in doing so, saved my life."

"Now it is your turn to save the life of this child."

"Do I *want* to save him? Is it dangerous?"

"Morgana is an enemy of Galhadria and mankind. Let me impress something upon you. Fail and we all may be doomed."

Jack Thane pointed to the wall behind and Peazle turned again. The frosting effect had gone and Peazle found himself looking into a bedroom decorated with posters of pop stars and model spaceships hanging on wires. The boy was sitting on his bed, head bowed, idly playing with two little chains around his neck. At the end of one chain dangled a little silver whistle. The other held a silver bear.

"Odd bits of jewellery," said Peazle. "Nice quality too," he added, betraying his expertise as a former crook.

"The boy does not realise it, but he holds the key to Morgana increasing her powers a hundredfold. Don't let that happen, Peazle."

Then the child on the wall raised his head and the pickpocket's eyes widened in recognition.

"Yes. I believe you met him once." The wizard smiled thinly.

"His name is Charlie Wilson."

The Wasteland

Charlie woke in an excellent mood, though it was muted by exhaustion, for it had taken him a long time to drift into sleep. He was delighted by his parent's unexpected attention and the possibility of leaving Fenton. What's more, it was Saturday and he wouldn't have to go to school and face Gary Macmillan. The day after, he would be in Birmingham with mum's friend Shirley. To settle down at last!

The boy was still uneasy about what he had seen in the garden. He might have dismissed it as a trick of the light, if he hadn't witnessed so many strange and frightening things last summer. Dragging himself wearily into the shower, he wondered if his life was ever going to be the same again.

He had no way of guessing things were about to get a hundred times worse.

The shower woke him properly and he got dressed and ran down the stairs to have breakfast. There was a note in the middle of the kitchen table, weighed down by a half-eaten sausage.

Off to the Job Centre. Don't go anywhere.
Love, Mum and Dad X.

"Rub it in, why don't you?" Charlie poured himself a bowl of cornflakes. He was by no means sure his father really wanted to work in a bank and didn't want to be eternally reminded of the sacrifice his parents were making to ensure he had a more stable life. Anyway, his mother and father would have discovered by now that the Job Centre was shut on a Saturday. Most likely, they'd have gone to the movies instead.

Before his summer escapade, Charlie would happily have obeyed his parents and spent a whole day on his PlayStation. Now he didn't feel like sitting at home in front of the TV when he could be out doing something. Trouble was, he lived in Fenton and there really wasn't anything to do. Charlie could either hang out in the little town square, where everyone would see he didn't have any friends - or go and explore the surrounding countryside. It was an easy choice to make. He put on his hiking boots, got a rucksack out of the cupboard and filled it with the meagre contents of the fridge. Charlie's parents weren't very big on food shopping.

On impulse, he turned his parent's note over and wrote on the back

Sorry. Gone to do something VERY important –
Charlie xxxx

He hadn't a clue what that important thing might be, but it sounded good. Then he shouldered the rucksack and let himself out the front door.

A few hundred yards up the street, a narrow alley between houses led onto a patch of wasteland, followed by a stretch of allotments. On the other side of the cultivation was a railway line and, beyond that, nothing but farmland and rolling hills.

He started walking in that direction, unaware he was heading into a trap.

Halfway down the street, he heard a rustling noise from behind the hedge he was passing. The gardens in his road were bordered by waist-high walls but this particular house had been empty for some time. The garden was choked with long weeds and fronds of unruly foliage tumbled over the crumbling brickwork. The bush nearest him rustled again. Charlie put his hands on the wall and peered over, trying to see what kind of animal was making the undergrowth tremble. Maybe there was something trapped. He leaned over further, trying to get a proper look.

"Get away from there!"

Startled, Charlie leapt back from the wall, whirling round to see who had shouted.

A boy stood at the end of the street, right in front of his house. Charlie had gone too far down the road to see him properly, but he could have sworn the stranger was wearing a bowler hat. He took a few hesitant steps towards the figure, which was now waving its arms wildly.

There was a roar from the other end of the street and Charlie spun again. Gary Macmillan and his two companions were racing towards him. They had been lying in wait behind a set of garages at the end of the road! The boy looked back towards his house, but the figure in the bowler hat was gone and the gap was closing rapidly between himself and the bullies, tearing up the deserted street.

The sensible thing would be to run back to his house, but what if he couldn't get the key in the lock before Macmillan reached him? What if the boy in the strange hat was part of the bully's gang and hiding in his garden? Making an instant decision, Charlie sprinted across the road and bolted down the narrow alley that led to the allotments. The alley twisted twice, and Charlie bounced off wooden fences in his haste to take each corner as fast as possible.

He shot out of the other end and onto the patch of wasteland. In front of him, ringed by a tall wall, strips of carefully tended land sloped steeply down to the rail line, each belt planted with rows of cabbages, strawberries and potatoes and dotted with garden sheds. A narrow path wound around the side of the allotment, beside a thick strip of high briar bushes, giving the plots some protection from the wind.

Charlie was about to take that route when he remembered that it ended in a high wire fence separating the lower reaches of the allotments from the railway at the bottom of the hill. The boy's parents had warned him never to climb the fence or cross the tracks, where express trains thundered past at deadly speed.

But staying on the path was just as dangerous, for it doubled back up the hill and came out at the far end of the waste ground, close to where it went down. If Macmillan followed him, while his sidekicks made for the other end, they would have him trapped.

What was the last thing Gary Macmillan would expect him to do? Apart from stand and fight, of course. He scanned the communal gardens quickly, looking for an alternative route - but the strips of carefully cultivated land offered no hiding place.

Unless!

In the closest allotment was a large, green compost bin. He remembered his parents' words. *Hesitation is an acrobat's worst enemy*. Without another thought, Charlie pulled open the lid. Inside were grass cuttings and torn up weeds, but they only came halfway to the top. He hauled himself inside and shut the top, just as Gary Macmillan and his gang burst out of the alley. Wrapped in sudden darkness, the boy curled himself into a ball and tried not to breathe too heavily - no mean feat, with rotting cabbage leaves tickling his nostrils.

Macmillan took in the allotments and the path with one glance. He motioned Watson and Brogan to circle the wasteland and ran off down the path, in the direction he was sure his quarry had gone.

Charlie stayed put, still trying to get his ragged breathing under control, listening to the fading footsteps of his pursuers. He guessed Macmillan would take a couple of minutes to reach the bottom of the hill and, by that time, Brogan and Watson would be far away as well. Then he could leap out of the bin and make a dash for his house. Wrapped in oppressive darkness, he counted silently, trying to judge the best moment to break for freedom.

Gary Macmillan was halfway down the incline, panting with exertion, when he came upon a boy sitting among the brambles. The stranger was small and wiry and wore a brightly coloured waistcoat and bowler hat.

"What you looking at?" Gary Macmillan snarled, his standard opening line for any new person he met. The boy didn't reply.

"Has anybody come past in the last few minutes?" The bully advanced threateningly on the stranger, to emphasize the fact he wasn't going to stand for silence, evasion or lies. The boy didn't seem too concerned.

"Not a soul," he replied calmly, hands in pockets. "Though I did see a child climbing into that green compost bin, way up there. Which, I must say, was a tad unusual."

He nodded to his right and Macmillan followed the gesture with his eyes. There was a clear view of Charlie's hiding place, further up the hill.

Gary Macmillan wasn't the type to trust anybody, especially someone wearing a flowery waistcoat. His hand shot out and grabbed the smaller boy's arm.

"You come with me and we'll check," he said. "If you're lying…"

He left the sentence unfinished, but there wasn't much doubt about what he would do if the bin turned out to be empty. The boy shrugged and calmly let the bully escort him up the path. Macmillan let out three piercing whistles as he walked. Watson and Brogan heard the call and hurried back. Both accomplices had armed themselves with sturdy fence posts.

"You sure you three are going to manage against one wee lad?" the stranger remarked casually, eyeing the vicious looking weapons. Gary Macmillan shot the boy a warning look.

"Keep hold of him," he motioned to Brogan, while he picked up a rock. "We'll shut his smart mouth in a minute."

The boy with the bowler hat and colourful waistcoat shrugged again.

The Cat Palug

Charlie was finding it harder and harder to breathe inside the compost bin. The lid of the container was almost airtight, the smell of rotting vegetation over-powering, and he could feel tiny bugs beginning to crawl over his face and into his sleeves. He was certain his asthma was about to play up. Surely the bully was far enough away for him to leap out and make his escape? He tensed his muscles and got ready to heave the lid open and dash for freedom.

Something crashed against the side of the container and it tilted precariously to one side, before settling back with a thump. Charlie gasped in terror and inhaled a mouthful of grass. As he tried to dislodge the lid, spluttering and coughing in panic, the side of the container buckled. This time the bin toppled over with a crash, the lid flew open and Charlie was catapulted out, along with an avalanche of half-rotted vegetation. The boy's fingers scrabbled frantically in freshly tilled soil and he scrambled to his feet, eyes wide with terror.

He saw Gary Macmillan and his henchmen, but they were almost twenty feet away. And, between him and the bullies, was a sight that defied reason.

It looked like a cat, but larger than any feline the boy had ever seen. Its ears were set back flat on a spade-shaped head, and its eyes were not almond-shaped but rounded, like those of a human. It was sitting up on powerful back legs that ended in viciously clawed feet. It was obvious that the creature, not the bullies, had tipped over the compost bin. Gary Macmillan and his sidekicks, coming through the allotment gate, stopped in their tracks, their faces mirroring Charlie's fear.

Instead of front legs, the cat had arms. Arms that ended in wide, hairless hands.

"Oh my God," breathed Watson. It was the first time Charlie had ever heard him speak.

The cat creature whirled round in surprise, its ears angling forward. It gave an evil hiss, like a sputtering fuse. The bully's henchmen took several steps back, their faces even paler than normal.

Gary Macmillan didn't have many virtues but he certainly wasn't short of courage.

"What are you looking at?" he snarled at the creature, though his voice was a lot higher than normal. Then he launched his rock at it. The cat gave a high-pitched wail and sprang towards them, spitting and snarling. Out of habit, more than any sense of bravado, Brogan and Watson leapt forward to defend their leader, swinging the jagged fence posts at the creature. It flailed its powerful arms, knocking the weapons aside. Macmillan bent quickly and picked up another rock. From behind the bullies a small figure, one Charlie hadn't noticed in the confusion, darted around the battle and sprinted over. As he approached, Charlie got a proper look at his face.

"Peazle?" he gasped.

"Glad to make your acquaintance, once more." The boy doffed his bowler politely. "Now run."

He grabbed Charlie by the arm and pulled away. The bullies, swiping wildly at the hissing cat, didn't notice their prey was escaping.

Charlie and Peazle sprinted, stumbling and gasping, onto the wooded path and headed towards the railway track. Halfway down the slope, Charlie looked back, in time to see Gary Macmillan and his sidekicks fleeing into the alley. Brogan's torn shirt was flapping wildly and Macmillan's arm hung limply by his side. There was no sign of the monster.

"Faster!" Peazle hissed. "That thing doesn't want them, or they'd be dead. It wants you."

He reached the bottom of the hill and launched himself at the high wire fence that cordoned off the railway track, climbing swiftly to the top and reaching down for his companion.

"I can't cross the railway line," Charlie shouted. "I'm not allowed. It's dangerous!"

"You think *that* creature isn't dangerous?" Peazle yelled back, hauling at the boy. "What do you suppose it's after you for? A kiss?"

He toppled over the top of the mesh fence, grabbing Charlie's collar and pulling him along. Charlie lost his grip, almost plummeting down the other side and onto the track. Peazle caught the boy and pressed him against the wire until he could get a proper handhold. The pickpocket was a lot stronger than he looked.

They leapt down onto the railway embankment as the creature exploded out of the undergrowth. It hit the fence with such ferocity Charlie thought it would scythe right through. The chain link rattled violently but didn't give. The cat creature glared maniacally at Charlie, only inches away, lips curled back into its stubby face and spittle drooling from snarling fangs.

Then it began to climb.

"Come on!" Peazle pulled Charlie away from the fence, where he had been transfixed by the creature's stare. "Up the other side, for God's sake. Or it will be upon us!"

He ran across the tracks and leapt onto an identical wire fence on the other side. Charlie went after him. His legs felt as if they were jelly and his arms seemed to have lost the power to pull him up. The creature was almost at the top of the first fence, which it had scaled in a fraction of the time the boys had taken. It let out a howl of triumph. Except...

It wasn't a howl. It was the wail of a train.

Seconds later, the Birmingham express rounded the corner. The creature somersaulted over the top of the fence in a perfect arc, using powerful arms the way a gymnast would. As it landed on the other side, the train swept past, obscuring the cat from the boys' view. The chain of the fence rattled and swung, and Charlie had to use all his remaining strength to stop himself being plucked off his perch and sucked under the thundering wheels.

"Will you get up here!" Peazle reached down and grabbed his companion by the hair. "A train isn't going to stop it!"

He yanked violently and Charlie scrambled after him, wincing in pain. In a few seconds, they were over the top and plummeting down the other side. The boys hit the ground as the last carriage of the express whizzed past. Suddenly visible again, the cat-creature bounded across the tracks and began to rapidly scale the second fence.

"We can't outrun it!" Charlie sobbed.

"We don't have to." Next to the fence was a narrow road lined with more bushes. Peazle dived into the nearest thicket and hauled out a mass of shiny chrome. "I always plan ahead."

"Bikes?" Charlie gasped.

"What were you expecting? A helicopter?" Peazle vaulted onto one bike and held out the other. The creature was already on the top of the second fence, so the boy jumped onto the proffered cycle and began to pump, the pedals, gathering speed. The cat hit the ground and lurched towards them. It moved with awkward but speedy lunges, using massive forearms to pull itself along, knuckles folded, swinging its short legs under the furry torso, the way an ape would. Now it was Peazle who was in trouble, his bike wobbling as he tried desperately to keep it under control.

"What's the matter?" Charlie yelled over his shoulder.

"I grew up in the 19th century! I'm not exactly used to bicycles!"

The pickpocket was veering from one side of the road to the other, the creature only yards behind.

"That's what you call planning ahead?" Charlie groaned.

Peazle ignored him, putting his head down and pedalling furiously, grim determination etched on his face. The creature leapt, arms outstretched, but the bike straightened and shot forward. The cat missed him by inches, landing heavily and rolling across the tarmac. The pickpocket steadied his handlebars at last and the two boys gathered speed, leaving the creature, gasping and spitting, rolling on the tarmac behind.

"Nothing to it," Peazle cried gleefully. "All I had to do was find the scientific principle behind these velocipedes. Pedal like hell."

He grinned as the bikes crested a rise and the boys soared down the hill and away from danger. "Course, it helps to have a Cat Palug chasing you."

"A what?" Charlie panted breathlessly, the wind whistling through his thick hair.

"A Cat Palug." Peazle waved behind him, though the creature was now too far away to see. The bike wobbled dangerously again and the pickpocket quickly returned both hands to the handlebars.

"I suppose I have some explaining to do."

"You think?" Charlie changed gears. "I'd certainly say so."

Waiting for the Train

After a couple of miles hard pedalling, they came upon a bus stop and Peazle slammed on the brakes. The bike went into a violent skid and vanished into a ditch. The pickpocket emerged a few moments later, pulling twigs from his hair. He fished a large fob watch from his pocket and glanced at it.

"You should dump your bicycle too," he said, as if his loss of control had been meticulously thought out. "The autobus will be here any minute."

Right on cue, the blue and white bulk of a Birmingham corporation bus appeared in the distance.

"We're getting a bus?"

"Faster than a bicycle. That creature behind does not tire, like you and me. Do not think, for a moment, it has given up the chase."

Peazle held out his hand and waved down the approaching vehicle. The bus ground to a halt and its double doors slid open.

"I hope you have some money."

"Where are we going?" Charlie dropped a handful of coins into the driver's palm as the pickpocket ushered him inside. The other passengers stared at their dishevelled appearance or, perhaps, Peazle's outland-ish bowler hat and waistcoat.

"My parents will be back soon." Charlie protested. "They'll wonder where I am."

"Right now, the Cat Palug is wondering where you are too. That's what is praying on my mind."

Peazle and Charlie sat down and the pickpocket looked nervously at the open bus door. Finally, it hissed shut and the vehicle pulled away.

"What was that thing?" Charlie whispered.

"A Cat Palug? One of the dark creatures of old. I doubt anyone has seen one for hundreds of years." Peazle shook his head in disbelief. "Yet it came right into a town to get you."

"I should go back. Tell my mum and dad."

"Tell them what?" Peazle laid a hand on his friend's shoulder. "That you were attacked by a moggie with hands?"

He looked out of the window nervously.

"Even if they believed you, nobody else would. Then you'd all be in mortal danger."

"How do you know Gary Macmillan and his gang didn't scare it off? They scare most things off."

"Those boys we left behind?" Peazle dismissed the idea with a wave of his hand. "They're only alive be-cause three youths mauled to death in a little place like this would draw too much attention to the thing that killed them."

"But they saw it. They'll tell."

"Would you believe, if you hadn't witnessed it?" The pickpocket tried to wipe away the grime that covered the window but only succeeded in smearing it around. "Besides, I get the feeling those young gentlemen are not known for telling the truth."

Charlie could see the logic in that.

"I'm sorry, my friend." Peazle dejectedly scrubbed at the large stripe of dirt that now adorned his sleeve. "The only way to keep you and your parents safe is to get as far away as possible."

"Got anywhere in mind, or are we just fleeing in general?"

"I thought I'd explain once we were on the train." The pickpocket pushed his face against the pane and tried to see past the muck.

"The train?" Charlie grabbed his companion and pulled him around. "What are you talking about? I'm not taking any train."

Peazle stared at him with eyes that seemed sad, tired and very old. But then, he was old, Charlie remembered. Though he still looked like a boy, the pickpocket had been alive for almost two centuries.

"There are dark creatures hunting you, Charlie. They have been sent by Morgana, last of the Gorrodin Rath. We must flee."

"Wait a minute!" Charlie shook his head vehemently. "*Mordred* was the last of the Gorrodin Rath." He gave a shiver. "I killed him,"

"Morgana is Mordred's mother," Peazle said flatly. "And far more deadly."

Charlie went white.

"That's why she's after me? Because I killed her son?"

"You're not exactly her favourite person," Peazle agreed. "Yet, that is not the reason she is hunting you."

He leaned close and whispered in the boy's ear.

"She is looking for the cup."

"The only cup I've got has a picture of the X Men on the side. I bought it in Woolworths."

"The Grail cup. The source of her power."

"*I* don't have it. I don't even know what it is."

"I believe you," the pickpocket said. "Yet you are the only lead Morgana has, for the cup was stolen from her by a certain young girl."

He shrugged.

"And you were the last person to see her."

"Her?"

"Yes," Peazle replied evenly. "Morgana is searching for your friend Lilly."

Charlie sat in miserable silence, glaring past Peazle at the gritty window. Ploughed fields and hedgerows, flickering past gaps in the dirt, were gradually being replaced by the red bricks and trimmed gardens of Birmingham's suburbs. He had the horrible feeling that his old life was passing away like the greenery. He pulled his mobile phone from his jacket pocket and began to dial.

"At least I can call my parents," he said brightly. "Let them know what's going on."

He stopped dialling and smiled sarcastically at Peazle.

"Once I work out exactly what *is* going on."

"Ah! A mobile telephone. Don't get it near my head." The boy gingerly took the phone from Charlie and studied it. "Amazing! Though I must admit, I am puzzled by this modern desire to send text messages. I thought the telephone was invented so people could talk to each other."

He reached up and pushed the mobile through the open ventilation window.

"What are you doing?" Charlie jumped to his feet, but the phone had already shattered into a hundred pieces on the road behind.

Peazle seized Charlie's arm and gripped hard. Grimacing in pain, the boy was forced down into his seat.

"Listen to me, Charlie!" Peazle hissed. "Listen well! Morgana will think nothing of using your parents as bait to get to you. Do you understand?"

He squeezed tighter and the boy winced again.

"She hopes to use Lilly to find the cup. She hopes to use you to find Lilly. And she will use your parents to get to you. Morgana is following a trail. A cold one, certainly, but these are the clues she has. Your mother and father are only safe as long as you don't communicate with them!"

"I've no idea where Lilly is." Charlie blinked back tears. "This isn't fair."

"I know that only too well." The pickpocket let go of Charlie's arm and stared angrily out of the window once more. "That's life, though."

The low, spacious houses had now gone and high-rise flats and factory chimneys signalled they were entering the heart of the city.

"You've risked your life twice to save me," Charlie said. "Once last summer and once today." The corrugated roof of Birmingham train station slid into view, visible through the narrow gap between the grime and the top of the window. "But, come on, Peazle! I can't just leave my parents not knowing where I am."

"Their anguish will surely be great," the pickpocket agreed. "So Morgana will sense this, know they are not in touch with you and leave them be."

The bus shuddered to a stop.

"You and I have both seen Mordred." The pickpocket whispered, narrowing his eyes. "Do you really want your mother and father to come face to face with his kin?"

Charlie stood, breathing heavily.

"Let's go," he said shakily. "We've got a train to catch."

The Policemen

Charlie's mother and father had only been home for minutes when the doorbell rang. To their surprise, two policemen stood on the front steps.

"Mr Wilson.?" The lead policeman was short and portly, with a small black moustache. He looked a bit like a traffic warden who had put on the wrong uniform.

"Yes?"

"I'm Sergeant Plune and this is Constable Valentine. I'm sorry to disturb you, but we're investigating a rather strange report." The policemen looked uneasily at each other. "See, eh… we picked up a trio of young boys a short while ago. They were covered in bruises and lacerations. Some of them rather serious."

The policeman rubbed his forehead, unsure of how to proceed.

"The kids seemed rather… eh… hysterical. They… um… claimed they'd been attacked by a large cat."

"A cat?"

"A cat, yes." The policemen looked at each other again. "According to the boys, a cat with hands."

"A cat with hands." Now it was Mr and Mrs Wilson's turn to look at each other.

"Excuse me, officer," Charlie's dad looked puzzled. "Cats don't have hands."

"Yes, I know that." The policeman was growing visibly more uncomfortable. "Thing is, they say your son was a witness."

"Was he hurt?" Charlie's mother pushed past her husband.

"No, madam. Apparently, he got away. Now, normally, we wouldn't pay any attention to such a wild tale - but the boys' injuries are quite serious. Is there any way we could talk to your son? Get his side of the story."

The policemen looked as if they were ready to continue the conversation inside the house, but Charlie's mother didn't move from the doorway.

"He isn't here, right now," Charlie's father said. "Of course, we'll call you as soon as he comes home."

"Any idea where he might be?"

"Out playing, I suppose." Charlie's father shook his head. "He's a very sensible boy, though. I'm positive he wouldn't be involved in anything… naughty."

"I'm sure he wasn't. But we *would* like to talk to him." Plume removed his hat and polished the brim. "One boy's arm was broken in four places. Never seen injuries quite like it." He replaced the hat and shadows hid his eyes again. "We'd just like to get to the bottom of this."

"Of course, officer." Charlie's mum gave an inno-cent smile. "Like my husband said, we'll give the local station a ring as soon as he appears."

"No need, madam." The taller officer at the back spoke for the first time. "This house is on our beat. We'll be back in a couple of hours. Sort it out then."

"Of course." Charlie's father seemed dazed. "But a cat with hands? How ridiculous."

"Ridiculous. Yes. Of course. I'm sure your son can clear it all up." The officers nodded gravely and walked back down the garden path.

Charlie's father closed the door behind them. Char-lie's mother was already running for the kitchen, her face white. She snatched a note from the table and held it up.

Gone to do something VERY important – Charlie
xxxx

Charlie's father was heading up the stairs, three at a time.

"Where are you going?" she called.

"To get coats," he said. "We're going to look for our boy."

Charlie sat in a dark corridor at the back of the rail-way station, sandwiched between a broken photo booth and a pile of empty boxes. He had cleaned up as best he could in the station washroom, and was now eating the Cornish pasty he'd packed in his rucksack - though his mouth was too dry to enjoy the taste. A few feet away, crowds jostled in and out of fast food bars, streaming towards and away from their trains. The air was filled with chattering and shouting and charged with all the emotions of a mass of humanity saying hello and goodbye. The boy looked down. His hands were shaking so badly that bits of pastry were strewn in a circle around him.

Peazle emerged from a crowd of suited commuters. He crouched next to Charlie and flourished two tickets in his face.

"The train for Edinburgh leaves in ten minutes. I got us first class too."

"Best to go on the run in comfort, eh?" Charlie whistled sarcastically. "Where did you get the money for that?"

"I am a master pickpocket, you know." Peazle cocked his head and listened to the distorted mumbling coming from the loudspeaker overhead. "Two centuries of technological advancements, and you still haven't figured out a way to make station announcements intelligible."

"If you don't tell me why we're going to Edinburgh, you won't be intelligible either." Charlie grabbed his companion by the waistcoat. "Cause you'll have my fist in your mouth."

"I have arranged to meet my master there."

"Your master?"

"As you know, I live in the land of Galhadria now," Peazle sighed. "Galhadria is ruled by a circle of great sorcerers. The Lords of the Western Wilderness they call themselves."

"That's pompous."

"They're mighty wizards, not some Rotary club." Peazle tucked one of the train tickets into Charlie's pocket. "I work for Jack Thane, the most powerful of the Lords. You met him briefly."

"And he sent you?"

"Jack Thane has no desire to see a monster like Morgana gain more power." The boy gave a half-hearted smile. "So he told me to rescue you."

"You're not exactly the seventh cavalry." Charlie looked through his fingers at the small figure seated opposite him. "Unless you have a cunning plan."

The pickpocket shrugged modestly. "You know what a Thin Place is?"

"It's a gateway to Galhadria."

"Yes. There are only a few open Thin Places left in this country, and most are in desolate parts of the north. But there is one in Edinburgh."

"In Greyfriars Graveyard? Yeah. I saw it once."

"We will go there and you will retreat to the safety of Galhadria."

"What!"

"It's only for a little while."

"And what are *you* going to do?"

"Find Lilly. She's the next link in the chain. Then, hopefully, the cup itself. Once it is safe in Thane's deepest stronghold, Morgana will have more to worry about than chasing after some small boy."

The pickpocket gave a wide smile.

"You'll be able to return to your parents." He prised Charlie's hands loose and helped the boy to his feet. "But we're not safe yet. We have to leave straight away."

"Are you sure Lilly has this stupid cup?" Charlie brushed the last crumbs from his jeans and slung the rucksack over his shoulder. "Or even knows where it is?"

Across the platform, a grimy locomotive gave a dragon-like hiss and backed out of the station, its clacking staccato growing more confident as it gathered speed.

"The cup belonged to Lilly's father but had fallen into in the hands of the Gorrodin Rath." Peazle was looking awkwardly at him. "Few people could have stolen it from them. Lilly did."

The pickpocket leant in close to Charlie's ear, as if he were ashamed to say it.

"After all, she's Morgana's child too."

The Potion

Being on the train was a lot better than travelling by bus. The first-class compartment was almost empty and the seats were huge and smelled faintly of after-shave. Best of all, the windows were clean and the boys had a clear view of fields, rivers and towns clattering past.

Peazle would have been content to stare out of the window all day. He had never been on a train. The Galhadrians had no railways, happy to walk or ride steeds wherever they needed to go. They were immortal, after all, and felt they had all the time in the world.

Charlie allowed his companion to gaze across the landscape while he ordered coffee and Kit-Kats from a passing trolley. The boys silently sipped their steaming drinks and Charlie nibbled on a chocolate bar.

"Yes?" Peazle turned away from the view.

"I'd like to know how my friend's mother turned out to be a monster that's looking for me." He wiped his mouth with a napkin. "Lilly neglected to mention it."

"It's hard to know where to begin." The pickpocket took another sip of his drink. "I never actually tasted this coffee stuff before. It's making my hair stand on end."

"Start at the beginning."

"All right," Peazle nodded. "What do you know of the Gorrodin-Rath?"

"Nothing I like."

"Bear with me." The boy formed a triangle with his fingers and tried to look learned. "What do you know of their history?"

"Only what Lilly told me. Do you remember her at all? She was alive when you lived in Edinburgh too, but you knew her as Heather."

"Yes." Peazle thought back to the 19th century when he and his friend Duncan stayed in Edinburgh's underground city. "She was Duncan's friend more than mine, though he did not know she was an immortal."

"She didn't tell me much." Charlie, too, was recalling when he had first met Lilly. "Said her father was a great magician called Gorrodin, who lived in Galhadria hundreds of years ago. He... went bad, I suppose you'd say. Abandoned Lilly, left Galhadria and created an evil race on earth called the Gorrodin-Rath."

"Go on."

"They were trapped in underground caverns by a knight called Arturius. Gorrodin fled and hasn't been seen since. You killed most of the surviving Gorrodin-Rath and I got the last one eight months ago."

He drained his coffee and crumpled the cup with a flourish.

"End of story. Or so I thought."

"It's not the end of the story." Peazle sighed. "It isn't even the right story."

"Lilly wouldn't make up something horrible like that." Charlie felt an unexpected lurch in his stomach. "Not about her own dad."

He hesitated.

"Would she?"

"Lilly doesn't *know* the truth." Peazle scratched his chin uncomfortably. "But you need to, if you're going to help her."

"So, what *is* the truth?"

"Jack Thane gave me this." He reached into his pocket and pulled out a small phial of thick green glass with a wax stopper. "Drink it. It will allow you to see into the past and know what really happened all those centuries ago. It's not as nice as coffee, though."

Charlie nodded, not particularly surprised.

"Lilly pulled a similar trick on me when I first met her. That's how I knew so much about your adventures back then."

"My escapades pale beside what you're about to witness." Peazle snapped his fingers at a passing conductor. "Another of those truly excellent beverages, my good man."

He turned back to Charlie and reached for his Kit-Kat.

"Drink some potion. I already know the story, so I'll stick to coffee."

Charlie uncorked the phial and took a swig.

"Aaaaaaaaaargh! It tastes like medicine." He grabbed Peazle's cup, took a gulp and recoiled. "*How* many sugars are in this?"

"Lilly was right about one thing," the pickpocket continued. "Gorrodin was indeed her father - and one of the greatest wizards in Galhadria. At one time, he was also a Lord of the Western Wilderness." He took a sip, shrugged, and added another sachet of sugar.

"He was alive in the days when Galhadrians walked on earth and long before that. When the Little People finally withdrew to their own world, he was one of the few still free to visit mankind."

"What's Galhadria like?" Charlie interrupted.

"Eh?"

"You've been living there ever since you were taken. What's it like?"

"It's an awful lot better than the place I came from." Peazle shrugged. "Rolling hills, snowy peaks, vast forests - that kind of thing."

He gestured out of the window, where a wooded incline swept majestically down to a stream below. Half a pram and two litter bins protruded from the water.

"Looks a bit like earth, without the pollution and overcrowding."

Charlie looked out. The gorge had been replaced by row after row of identical houses, grey pebble-dash below each window stained with dark patches, as if they spent most of their time crying.

The boy turned quickly away from the sight.

"Go on," he said.

"Gorrodin had a fondness for mankind, though they were little more than savages at that time. I mean, we're talking hundreds of years ago. One day it occurred to him, he might help humans be better than they were. In the area now known as southern Scotland, he gathered together the bravest and noblest of the race and forged them into a tribe."

"Hold on!" Charlie tapped on the table. "I thought Galhadrians didn't interfere in the lives of humans?"

"Absolutely," Peazle nodded enthusiastically. "The other Lords were furious. But Gorrodin was a powerful sorcerer and the best they could do was banish him."

"To the place where he wanted to be, anyway?" Charlie said mockingly. Both boys giggled.

"Yes, he wasn't too concerned," Peazle said. "But things got out of hand."

He stopped laughing and carried on.

"Gorrodin's tribe flourished. Everyone was equal there, a beacon of light in what came to be known as the Dark Ages." The pickpocket was obviously warming to his story - but Charlie noticed the boy's voice was starting to sound a little thin - and he looked slightly blurred. Charlie wondered if that was the potion or the effect of drinking Peazle's coffee.

"The magician appointed a human leader, Arturius, to rule his tribe, warriors dedicated to bringing peace to the land. Their home was called Taneborc, roughly where Edinburgh is now. Arturius is now better known as King Arthur and Taneborc drifted into legend as Camelot."

Charlie shook his head, trying to clear it, but the scenery outside the window seemed to be melting and reforming. He knew it was Thane's magic at work, so he surrendered to its spell.

Dirty factories faded away and he could suddenly see a large thatched village, surrounded by a barrier of raised logs. Smoke rose from a communal fire in a central clearing, a series of long wooden outhouses held pigs and cattle and, on a distant hill, there stood a stone fort.

Out of the corner of his eye, he could see a cloud of dust rising behind a glittering column of riders, cantering out of the distance towards the village. There was a flurry of shouted activity and the gates of the stockade swung open for the approaching horsemen.

"All legends have a grain of truth at their centre, and the legend of King Arthur is no different." Peazle's voice came far away now. "You ought to know that, more than anyone."

Charlie was no longer listening. His body was still on the train but his mind was swooping over the emerald fields towards Camelot. He noticed a white hawk with black-tipped wings sailing alongside him and knew, from past experience, that birds like these were the eyes of the Galhadrians, keeping watch.

The conductor arrived with more drinks and stared questioningly at the motionless boy.

"He always sleeps with his eyes open. Weird, isn't it?"

Peazle smiled at the astonished official and emptied four sachets of sugar into his new cup.

Mordred

Charlie found himself floating into a wooden chamber at the centre of the stockade. Smoke wafted up from a cooking fire through a hole in the thatched roof. At one end was an enormous round table circled by seated warriors.

A man strode into the building, smiling broadly, and raised a gloved hand in greeting. He was tall and broad, not long into his twenties, yet he bore himself with confidence and dignity. Around his muscular shoulders hung a bearskin, held at the throat by a silver Roman clasp and a short sword hung on his waist. Behind him stood two warriors. One was even taller, with a ring of fiery red hair and moustache to match. The other was older, grey streaking the thin hair that bordered his sallow face. The young man bent his knee briefly to the packed earthen floor, then stood. A woman with short black hair and pretty features emerged from the shadows. She grinned and gave the newcomers a little wave.

At the opposite end of the room a short, stocky knight rose at the table, a plain circlet of gold resting on his forehead. He, too, was young, but his bright blue eyes were edged with dark creases, the mark of a man who carried more responsibility than his years warranted.

"Welcome home, Mordred, my friend," he said warmly. "News of your victory has preceded you."

Charlie drew a sharp breath at the mention of the newcomer's name.

"My Lord Arturius." Mordred acknowledged the compliment with a brief nod. "We met the Pictish army at Longmuir and crushed them. Our northern borders are safe."

He unfastened the bearskin and swept it over his shoulder.

"Uallabh. Pelinore. Take your places with our comrades."

The two companions sought out empty spaces at the table. Those on each side slapped their backs and pushed food and drink into eager hands. Arturius raised his goblet and winked at Mordred.

"Peace in our times," he said. The other knights held up their goblets in agreement and swallowed heartily. Mordred raised his cup, but merely sipped. The action did not escape the man sitting to the right of Arturius. He was older than most of his companions, though his actual age was impossible to determine. Like the king, his eyes were disturbingly bright - green rather than blue - matching the cloak that covered his torso.

"You are troubled after such a victory, Mordred?" he said softly.

"In truth, Gorrodin, I am," Mordred replied. "The Picts are a warlike race and I feel that this defeat will merely fuel their hatred."

He swallowed his drink half-heartedly.

"I worry that, years from now, my sons will still be fighting our battles. All in the name of peace."

Gorrodin nodded and stroked his long chin. He was one of the few clean-shaven men at the table.

"You think I should use my magic to destroy the Picts forever, young friend? Aye and subdue the Angles and Britons in the south. In fact, anyone else who threatens us?"

Mordred nodded enthusiastically and several others at the table banged the wood in agreement. Gorrodin glanced around and held up a hand.

"You will always have enemies, as long as violence, selfishness and greed fester in the hearts of men. Would you have me banish all those too? Would you want me reaching inside everyone, without permission, and making whatever changes I please?"

A portly knight named Bahlain let out a belch of protest and several of his companions began to laugh.

"Say, for instance, I didn't like people being rude while I was trying to make a point."

Gorrodin swept a hand through the air and the laughter stopped instantly. Battle-hardened warriors looked at each other in astonishment and growing fear. Their mouths were open and full bellies shuddering, but no sound came from their lips.

The room was deathly silent.

The wizard clicked his fingers and gasps of shock and amazement shuddered through the hall, as the men found they could speak again.

"If I alter your world too much, it becomes *my* world," he said to the hushed men. "You must change it yourselves, I'm afraid. And you can - for your own Lord Arturius, who I call Arthur, has more greatness in his heart than my magic can ever match."

He suddenly looked humble.

"You all do."

The Knights of the Round Table were neither philosophers nor politicians, yet this was a sentiment they understood. As one man, they rose and toasted Arthur, then Mordred and each other. Arthur walked around the table, nodding to each man, then sat beside Mordred.

"This seems to be going well," he said.

Mordred grunted, then brightened as the woman who had waved earlier approached.

"A clever trick by Gorrodin, I thought," she said, brandishing a half-eaten chicken leg and wiping her lips daintily. "I always wanted to see the round table quiet for once."

"I am glad you are amused, mother. However, I fear it was an empty speech by your wizard, for all its cleverness." Mordred took the chicken leg and bit into it. "If you two weren't romancing, I'd have argued him into the ground."

The woman snorted.

"Not so empty, I fear." Arthur was suddenly solemn.

"My Lord?" Mordred asked quizzically.

"Gorrodin is right," Arthur said. "We must prove we can create a better world without the waving of a magic wand."

He hesitated, then straightened his back.

"That is why Gorrodin is leaving us."

"I am going too." The woman looked at the ground. "For you know that I love him."

"And I, her." Gorrodin appeared from nowhere and laid a hand on Mordred's shoulder. The young warrior jumped, hand reaching instinctively for his weapon.

"I wish you wouldn't do that."

"Despite my youthful appearance, I am old beyond your understanding," the wizard said softly. "Yet I have never loved the way I love your mother, Morgana. As you pointed out, I could wave a hand and make you accept this. Instead, I ask for your blessing."

For the second time, Charlie drew a sharp breath. This woman was Morgana? He didn't understand, for he could see no threat from the charming figure standing in front of him.

Mordred stood slowly until he was level with the wizard. The two held each other's stare.

"You and I do not agree on many things, sorcerer," he replied. "But we concur that my mother is an exceptional woman - and I trust her judgement in everything."

Morgana flushed bright red. Mordred reached out and clasped Gorrodin's hand.

"You have my blessing."

"You will not be forgotten, my friend." Arthur looked around at the revellers, each one loyal, brave and true, if slightly drunk. Uallabh was standing on the table, plaid round his waist, proudly showing his neighbours a battle scar on his bottom.

"I have talked to my men and we are agreed that, in honour of your memory, we will take your name."

Arthur bowed.

"From this day, we shall be known as the Gorrodin-Rath."

The Picts

Charlie felt himself plucked from Taneborc and spirited across time and space, quickly and smoothly as a bird gliding through air. Again, there was the hawk with the black-tipped wings, hovering beside him.

They flew north for miles, heading years into the future, until they landed beside the window of a small but elegant stone dwelling. Behind the boy, a low and level moor rose gently to nudge a line of cliffs and a tall waterfall plumed from the rock, like a gigantic horse's tail.

He heard giggling coming from the other side of the house and stuck his head around the corner to see who it was.

There was Lilly, a couple of years younger than he remembered, playing with a small dog. Charlie quickly ducked his head back, though it was obvious by now he was merely a spectator and couldn't be seen.

He peered through the window pane into the glowing interior. He was fairly sure that 7th-century houses didn't have glass, or metal window catches, for that matter. This must be the home of the wizard, Gorrodin. Sure enough, the sorcerer was sitting at a table with

Morgana, her dark hair shimmering in the firelight's glow.

Gorrodin held a small wooden cup between his hands.

"Magic is a powerful force and it can warp and change those who try to master it," the man was saying. "For that reason, even great wizards keep their powers, not within themselves, but in a special talisman. This one belongs to me."

He tapped the side of the cup and silver liquid bubbled up inside, filling the vessel almost to the rim.

"I call it my Grail," he continued. He pushed the cup towards his wife, but his face was troubled. "Morgana… Our daughter Lilly has my blood in her veins, so she is magical too. We will outlive you by thousands of years and I cannot bear that thought. If you drink from this, you will be like us."

"I don't know if I want to live forever." Morgana stared at the innocent-looking beaker.

"Nobody lives forever." the wizard smiled softly. "But immortals do live a long, long time."

"Then I will drink, for one lifetime with you and our daughter is too short."

Morgana reached for the cup but Gorrodin laid his hand gently upon hers.

"After this, however, you must never touch the Grail again." He pulled nervously at his chin. "It is not yours to use."

"Of course." Morgana bowed her head but not before Charlie spotted the sad look in her eyes. Gorrodin noticed it too.

"That was not an insult," he continued. "Humans and magic must not mix. It is too strong and corrupts them in a most terrible way."

He lifted his wife's head and smiled at her.

"But I have no fear." He spread his hand in front of his wife's face, drawing it into a smile. "Look. I wave my hand and the power of the Grail is yours to command. Because I trust you never to use it."

Morgana lifted the cup and drank.

Charlie found the scene swinging away like a revolving mirror, only to be replaced by an almost identical one. Lilly was further away, but she was taller now and her dog was no longer a puppy. He glanced in the window. Morgana was sitting writing at the table. There was no sign of Gorrodin.

He heard a rumble in the distance that transformed quickly into the thunder of horse's hooves. Morgana's head lifted, a look of consternation on her face. She rose to her feet and headed for the door.

Charlie skirted the house and arrived at the front door at the same time as Morgana emerged into the sunlight. Her hands shot to her mouth as she spotted whooping horsemen galloping across the moor towards her daughter. Their faces were daubed with blue and all were heavily armed.

"Picts!" Morgana breathed. "A war party!"

Lilly had spotted the horsemen and was sprinting back towards the safety of the house - but it was obvious the horsemen would catch her before she reached shelter. Morgana was about to head for her daughter then, realizing the same thing, turned and darted back into the house. Charlie ran towards the girl before remembering he could do nothing to help.

"Fetch Gorrodin!" he shouted at the empty doorway. But, if the wizard were around, he would have already been defending his family. Lilly was still racing for the house. Her dog turned and bounded towards the attackers in a desperate attempt to save his mistress.

The hound didn't stand a chance. After a few desperate lunges, it vanished under the oncoming hooves.

Lilly skidded to a halt, rage written across her childish face. She stretched out her hands and the leading Pict was catapulted backwards off his steed. She thrust her arms forward again and another rider went down. The remaining Picts yelled louder and spurred their horses on - there were far too many in the raiding party for the girl's fledgling magical powers to stop.

Lilly turned to run again, but a wooden axe came hurtling through the air and embedded itself in her back. She fell forward onto the heather, a gout of blood erupting in the air.

Charlie sank to his knees, his face ghostly white.

With a triumphant whoop, the leading Pict dismounted his horse and advanced towards the dying girl.

He never reached her.

Charlie could not feel the force that rushed past him, nor did he understand what it was. All he saw was a rippling in the air and ferns and heather curling in on themselves, as if subjected to immense heat. The shimmering path reached the Picts, turning them instantly to black outlines that broke and drifted into the moorland.

Charlie whirled. Morgana stood in the doorway, holding Gorrodin's Grail. She ran to her daughter, still clutching the cup, and knelt beside her. With a shudder, Morgana pulled the axe from Lilly's back and placed her hand over the spurting wound. She drank from the cup again, whispering hysterically to herself. The blood pouring between her fingers instantly stopped and, when she removed her hand, her daughter's wound was gone. Lilly's shallow, laboured breathing evened out until it became deep and regular.

"Sleep, my child," Morgana whispered. "When you awake, you will forget this dreadful thing." She hesitated. "Nor will you remember I broke my sacred promise to your father and used his Grail."

She clasped, then unclasped, her fingers and a small, glinting object appeared in her hand. She fastened it around her sleeping daughter's neck.

It was a tiny silver whistle on a chain.

"If you are ever in trouble again, my daughter, blow the whistle and I will come."

She stroked Lilly's cheek, then rose and walked back to the house. Charlie paused to make sure the girl was all right, then trotted into the house after her mother.

Morgana was replacing Gorrodin's Grail on a shelf. As she let it go, her hand trembled. Then she reached out and stroked the wooden surface, as gently as she had touched her child moments before.

She turned and Charlie took an involuntary step back. For a brief second, he had seen something flicker in her eyes - a glint that had not been there before. A more experienced observer might describe it as the first kindling of lust, or desire without bounds. Charlie only had one word for it.

Evil.

The Break-In

Sergeant Plune and Constable Valentine returned to Charlie's house at the end of their beat, as promised. Fenton was a small rural town and didn't have a lot of crime, so the 'handy cat' - as they jokingly called it - had been the highlight of their day. The two men had spent most of their shift trying to figure out what had happened.

"I still say those kids were hallucinating. Experimenting with drugs," Constable Valentine opened the Wilsons' garden gate and the two policemen strolled up the path. "The Macmillan boy is never out of trouble."

"I've never seen a hallucination break anyone's arm." Sergeant Plune knocked briskly on the front door. "Could be they came across some weird animal that escaped from a zoo. I saw a red panda once on TV and it had little fingers and thumbs for climbing trees. Mind you, that was in China."

He knocked again and the front door swung gently open.

"Mr and Mrs Wilson?" The policemen peered into the dark hall. "Are you here?"

There was no reply. As their eyes adapted to the gloom, they noticed that the occupants' telephone table was lying on its side.

Motioning for his companion to follow, Sergeant Plune moved cautiously into the house, crossed the hall and opened the living room door. Constable Valentine heard the sergeant gasp and looked over his shoulder.

The room looked as if a tornado had cut through it. Bookcases and chests of drawers lay on their sides, contents spilling out over the floor. A storm of paper, ornaments and knick-knacks were strewn across the room. The policemen quickly unfastened their batons and Constable Valentine hurried up the stairs while Plune inspected the ruined living room. He noticed several items of jewellery lying on the floor next to the contents of an upturned box. This house hadn't been burgled. It had been torn apart during the process of a frantic search. Sergeant Plune picked a spangly pair of tights from the floor and gaped at them.

Valentine's head appeared over the bannisters above. His raised eyebrows told Plune the bedrooms were in the same state.

"Nobody up here. No sign of the kid or the mother and father."

"What the hell is going on?" Sergeant Plune turned to see Charlie's parents standing in the doorway, looking, open-mouthed, at the wreckage of their house. He quickly dropped the tights.

"Mrs and Mrs Wilson," he said. "Eh… any news from of your son?"

Charlie's parents shook their heads.

"Then I think we'd better call Birmingham main branch." Plune pulled out his police radio. "Don't touch anything up there," he shouted to Constable Valentine, then tapped the antennae thoughtfully against his teeth.

"This is a lot more serious than some damned cat."

Events were flowing past Charlie as if history were a river. He saw Morgana practising sorcery with the Grail whenever Gorrodin and her daughter were absent. To the boy, it was obvious that everything good about the woman was being consumed by the magic inside her. Gorrodin obviously could not, or would not, see it.

The scene melted and changed. Now Gorrodin and Morgana were having a furious argument. The wizard stormed out of the house, anguish screwing up his face, heading towards a cave near the waterfall. His wife strode after him, tears streaking her cheeks.

"You have deceived me, my love," he shouted. "You promised not to use the Grail!"

From a leather bag at his side, he withdrew the wooden cup.

"It pains me, but I must keep the talisman where you cannot touch it. I shall seal it in this cave."

He tossed the Grail into the darkness and chanted a few words. With a crumbling shudder, the sides of the crevasse began to grind shut. Morgana stood behind her husband, fists clenching and unclenching in desperation.

As the cave entrance grew narrower, she stretched out her arms, fingers wide. The Grail shot out of the tiny gap in the quickly closing walls and into her hands. Gorrodin turned, eyes wide, as Morgana thrust out her arms again. The wizard flew backwards like a rag caught in some violent gale, vanishing into the cave. His cry of anguished betrayal was cut off, as the rocky sides slapped shut.

Morgana sank to her knees, clutching the Grail, as if it were a lost child. Without a backwards glance at the place where her husband was now entombed, she rose to her feet and strode away across the valley.

Charlie heard a small sob and looked around.

Lilly had been watching the whole scene, hiding in the heather.

Charlie flew through time and space again, south to where Edinburgh would, one day, stand. They saw Morgana arrive at Camelot with the Grail and how her return threw Arthur's tribe into disarray. Many knights welcomed Morgana warmly, for Northumbrian tribes from the south and Picts from the north were continually attacking. The Gorrodin Rath sorely needed help.

Arthur, however, wished to have nothing to do with the Grail. What's more, he did not believe Morgana's explanation that Gorrodin had returned to Galhadria and entrusted her with its powers to use in the Rath's defence.

Mordred, on the other hand, was tired of fighting endless battles. He accepted his mother's ruse without question and was happy to use Morgana's magic to right the wrongs of the world. Reluctantly, Arthur took his most loyal followers and left.

And so, as Charlie looked miserably on, the round table was destroyed. Mordred, Morgana and their supporters drank from the Grail and tried to use its magic. Like Morgana, they became obsessed with their new powers.

Months ticked by like seconds and the boy watched, with mounting horror, as the Gorrodin-Rath began to change. The more they practised forbidden magic, the more it altered them. They slowly transformed into dark creatures, troll-like in appearance, who could not bear the light of day. They no longer farmed the land but retreated into underground caverns, emerging at night to seek the easiest food they could find. Their former race.

The Gorrodin-Rath had become cannibals.

Arthur slumped on a rough wooden throne, his face creased with lines of anguish. Charlie stood beside him, unable to do anything but watch. The flap of the tent opened and a warrior stepped inside and knelt.

"There is a young girl here to see you, my lord."

"I have no time for an audience with children."

"She claims to be Gorrodin and Morgana's daughter."

In an instant, Arthur was on his feet and hurrying outside, Charlie right behind. There, in the bustle and sun-dappled smoke of the knight's camp, stood Lilly. The girl was grimy and bedraggled but standing tall and proud, as the daughter of a wizard should, in the presence of her king.

"Are you really who you say?" Arthur began. Then his voice trailed off. One look at the girl's emerald eyes told him all he needed to know.

"What has happened to Gorrodin, child?" he said gently

"My father is trapped in a cave to the far north, my Lord, and I do not know how to free him. So I have sought you out. I am half Galhadrian and know the ways of the Little People, but my powers are still weak and the journey south was dangerous. I am truly sorry, but it has taken me many months to reach here."

Arthur crouched beside the girl and took her hand. Passing warriors stopped and looked in amazement at the sight.

"You must rest," he said. "We will talk once you have recovered."

Lilly shook her head.

"My anger burns too bright," she replied. "And it may be that I can aid you." She reached inside her tunic and brought out a lump of shining metal. "My father's race loved jewellery and finery, you see."

Arthur looked puzzled.

"When they abandoned earth, they left much behind, for Galhadria has no shortage of such treasures." The girl gave a small smile. "Not far from here, according to my father, was a hidden cache of fairy silver. I have found it for you."

"And?" Arthur looked none the wiser

"Fairy silver is deadly to dark creatures, the very things my mother and her followers have become. You have forges here, do you not?"

Comprehension began to dawn on Arthur's face and he nodded.

"Make weapons and armour from the silver," the girl continued. "If you strike without warning, you can enter the caves where the creatures live and rescue my father's Grail before they realise what is happening. It is the source of their power and they will be much weakened without it."

Arthur motioned to the gathering warriors.

"Assemble the men and have our blacksmiths stoke the campfires!" he shouted, flinging a cloak round his shoulders. "I want my warriors to form a raiding party. We will strike swiftly and take the cup."

He smiled warmly at the girl.

"Hope has come amongst us, at last."

The train whistle blew loudly and Charlie was back in the compartment again. He stared at Peazle, wide-eyed. The pickpocket blew on his coffee and tendrils of smoke ducked and curved around his lips.

"This wasn't the story Lilly told me!" Charlie stammered. "She claimed her father deserted her in Galhadria, went to earth and created a private army of monsters called the Gorrodin-Rath. She said her dad was the bad guy."

Peazle sipped his drink, staring awkwardly at his companion over the rim of the cup

"There is an explanation." The pickpocket looked grim. "But I fear you will not like it."

"No surprises there, then,"

The pickpocket drained the last of his coffee and looked solemnly out of the window again.

"We must be in Scotland," he said. "It's raining."

Charlie stared down at the stained Formica table. He felt sad and betrayed.

"Why did Lilly tell me some totally made-up story about Gorrodin leaving her?" he said finally. "Why didn't she never mention Morgana being her mother? Why didn't she go back and try to rescue her father?"

Peazle sighed heavily. He raised his hands ineffectually and put them back on the table again.

"Drink, my friend. You may as well know everything."

So, Charlie did.

The Last Stand of Arthur

Charlie found himself in the distant past, once more, standing on a dark, heather-covered escarpment, battered by rain. A line of mounted men looked warily up at the craggy hill in front of them. Cold rain was falling, plastering long hair to scalps and running down nervous faces. For a few moments, the rays of the setting sun burst through the clouds and danced across a bristling row of silver swords and spears.

The warriors struggled to control the horses, for the animals were rolling their eyes in fear, frantic hooves churning purple thistle heads into the mud. One horseman tugged powerfully at his reins, forcing his struggling mount closer to Arthur, who was marked out as their leader by the silver ringlet on his head.

"It is only moments till the sun sets, my lord," he cautioned. His long red hair was braided and his face daubed with a war mask of deep blue spirals. Charlie recognised him as the knight called Uallabh, made up for battle.

"Forgive me, sire, but I do not understand," he continued. "We have stolen back the cup. Are we to throw that advantage away by fighting in the dark and at the bottom of a hill? We could not be in a worse defensive position."

Arthur did not look round.

"The Gorrodin-Rath have become thieves, murderers and nightcrawlers," he said sorrowfully. "Only if they are sure of victory, will they commit their whole force to battle."

"And if they win?"

"By that time, the Grail will be gone. After all, I am entrusting one of my finest men to guard it."

The painted warrior was taken aback.

"My job is to fight with you, sire."

"The Grail must be kept from Morgana, old friend." Arthur looked unwaveringly into Uallabh's eyes. "I trust none but the greatest knight I have ever known."

Uallabh blinked rapidly, his jaw tight. He seemed about to speak again, but Arthur shook his head to cut him off. With a grunt, the warrior wheeled his horse around and stared angrily at Lilly.

The girl stood in the fading light, clutching her father's wooden cup. Arthur raised a gloved hand and pointed to his silent friend.

"Uallabh will get the Grail to safety," he smiled. "Even if he is none too pleased about it."

Then the sun slid behind the western hills. A long black shadow crept slowly over the small army and up the side of the hill, enveloping them in darkness.

"Listen."

At first, the men could hear nothing but the hiss of the rain and the whinnying of terrified horses. Then a sound like wind howling through a mountain pass drifted out of the darkness, growing louder and louder, until it was a nerve-shredding roar.

Shapes began to appear on the crest of the hill, black and monstrous. They almost blended into the darkness, were it not for the red glow of their eyes and the gleam of vicious fangs and teeth. Eventually, a solid mass of deformed bodies filled the horizon.

Arthur seemed calm and only those closest to him saw the knotted muscles of his jaw and the movement of his lips, as he uttered a silent oath.

Then he straightened, raised his spear and spurred his reluctant steed towards the enemy. Giving an inhuman scream, they rushed down the slope.

With a spirited war cry, Arthur's doomed army lifted their weapons and charged after him.

Charlie was whisked into the air and away from the carnage erupting below him, where monsters and men rushed together with a fury that made him screw shut his eyes. The moon raced across the sky, accompanied by the clash of steel and the screams of dying men and horses.

The boy floated down to the top of a nearby hill. Lilly and Uallabh were struggling towards him, almost blinded by the gusts of freezing rain soaking their clothes. The warrior swayed and stumbled, trying not to lean on the small figure, for the girl was already burdened by a leather bag slung over her shoulder. Uallabh's beard was matted with blood and a bronze breastplate hung half off his chest, bent and ripped as if it were tin foil.

They splashed, gasping, through a small stream – it was so dark they had not even seen it. The warrior sank to his knees and his shaking fingers fumbled at the breastplate fastenings until the ruined armour fell from his chest. Over the storm, the hiss of the stream, and his own ragged breathing, he could still hear the roar of battle drifting up from the valley below. Lilly looked back the way they had come and shuddered.

"I should still be down there, fighting alongside my comrades," the warrior rasped. He tried to rise, but his legs no longer supported him and he collapsed with a grunt of pain.

"No, Uallabh! We have to get away!" The girl clasped the warrior's quilted tunic and tried vainly to pull the man to his feet. "We have to get the Grail to safety!"

The jerkin fell open, revealing a deep, jagged wound running from the warrior's shoulder to his waist. Lilly looked quickly away and saw that a faint light was seeping into the sky from the east.

"It will be dawn soon." Tiny hands urgently clasped at the tunic again. "We only have to last a little longer."

A merciless roar shattered the night and Lilly's head shot up, eyes wide with fear, scanning the darkness. Uallabh's hand went to the knife at his side and he pulled himself to his knees by sheer force of will. A riderless horse, lathered with sweat and blood, thundered out of the night. Eyes rolling in terror, it swept past them and vanished into the darkness again.

"The creatures must be almost upon us," the warrior snarled. "You go. I will hold them off."

"The Gorrodin Rath are still in the valley, fighting with your companions. Only Morgana is following." The girl fished Gorrodin's wooden Grail from the leather bag, waved her hand over the top, and then thrust it at the warrior. "But my mother... a whole army will not stop her."

Uallabh looked down. Miraculously, liquid glittered inside the goblet, almost up to the rim.

"Drink from this," Lilly urged.

The warrior pushed the cup violently away.

"Never!" The warrior pushed the cup violently away. "I will not be tainted by its dark magic."

"Listen to me," the child whispered urgently. "You are noble and pure of heart, or you would not be here. You will stay that way if you do not attempt to use the powers the goblet gives you. I promise."

"What will it do to me?" the man asked.

"It will stop you ageing."

"I do not wish to be immortal."

"More importantly, it will cure your wounds. I need you!"

Uallabh looked intently at the child, his mouth set in a grim line. Finally, he reached out, took the cup and drank.

There was another horrendous roar, much louder now. The child took the goblet and stuffed it back into her bag. Uallabh tried to get up again and this time, to his astonishment, rose easily to his feet.

"Go north. Hide the Grail," Lilly said. "Then wait for me at the Glen of Rosslyn. No matter how long it takes."

The warrior took the bag and threw it over his own broad shoulder. He stood fully erect and his eyes were clear and hard.

"And if this… thing kills you?"

"It will not dare risk the Dolorous Stroke."

"The what, now?"

"I have no time to explain!"

"Then I will do as you ask." The man nodded once and strode away without a backward glance.

Lilly crouched down in the heather. The sky was definitely lighter now and it would soon be dawn.

A huge figure appeared out of the blackness.

The girl allowed a horrified hiss to escape her lips. In the months she had been travelling, magic had corrupted Morgana, until she was unrecognisable. She was almost twice the height of a man, with a torso so large and muscular, it was more beast-like than human. Malevolent eyes, deep in a knobbly skull, bobbed above a snarling mouth bristling with fangs. Blood dripped from a gaping wound in her abdomen.

Lilly raised her hands and a bolt of light shot from her fingers. It struck Morgana in the chest and threw her backwards into the heather. Seconds later, the creature was on its feet, unscathed by the blow. The thick white lips pulled back in a scornful sneer.

"You're too late," the girl said. "The Grail is gone and I do not know where."

"So, you too, hate me," Morgana snarled. "Would stop me from possessing what is rightfully mine."

A heavily taloned hand shot out, pointing at the little girl.

"Then let the man who caused this grief take the blame." The claws twitched and Lilly went rigid, as if some invisible hand had her by the throat.

"You will believe your father, the mighty Gorrodin, deserted you and caused all this misery." Her voice dripped with contempt at the mention of her husband's name. "You will forget me, for you are not worthy to be my daughter."

She opened her hand and the girl sank to the ground, unconscious.

"Sleep, Lilly," she whispered.

She looked around, sniffing the air. But Uallabh and the Grail were gone and dawn was breaking. With a roar of fury, she stretched her hands to the sky where the hawk still floated. With a screech, it plummeted from the sky in a ball of flame.

"And I do not like being spied on," she hissed.

Then she headed across the heather to find a place to hide and heal, leaving her minions to their fate.

Charlie sat up bolt upright, giving a small squeak.

"*That's* the thing chasing me?"

Peazle nodded.

"Her own mother?" he breathed. "Lilly's mother did that to her?"

"Lilly truly believes the story she told you," the pickpocket said. "She thinks her father caused the death of Arthur and the curse of hatred is heavy upon her."

The pickpocket looked solemnly out the window. A ruined castle slumped on a nearby hilltop, beaten into a shapeless pile of stones by the passage of time.

"Why didn't the Lords of the Western Wilderness come through a Thin Place," Charlie snapped. "To tell her the truth?"

Peazle's look of consternation changed to something that resembled anger.

"The Lords of the Western Wilderness always disapproved of Gorrodin meddling in human affairs. They were happy to see both him and the Gorrodin-Rath out of the way."

"I'm not going to like this." A horrible feeling grew in the pit of Charlie's stomach. "Am I?"

"Having Lilly stay under Morgana's enchantment suited the Lords well." The pickpocket swallowed hard, as if he had eaten something distasteful. "They let her keep watch over the remaining Gorrodin-Rath, waiting for her father to return to free them - so she could have her revenge." He sighed. "Though the Lords knew very well he was trapped for eternity."

"How could they do something so rotten?"

The conductor, passing by, gave them a dirty look, then hurried off before Peazle could ask him for more coffee.

"Lilly is only half Galhadrian. She's also half-human." The pickpocket looked ashamed. "The Little People do not care much for humans. They care even less for half breeds."

"And these are the guys you work for, eh?" Charlie shot back. "Well, I tell you what. I don't care much for Galhadrians.

"To be honest with you, Charlie," Peazle grunted. "I don't either."

Inspector Archer

The train was travelling along the coastline when Peazle spotted the grey mass that was the city of Edinburgh, twenty miles away, on the other side of a curving bay. Charlie had been silent for a long time, taking in all that Peazle had told him. The pickpocket stared glumly at the sparkling water. He knew his companion must be in turmoil and had no idea how to ease his anguish.

"What I don't understand," Charlie said, as if on cue. "Is why Morgana has waited all this time to go after the Grail again."

"I've got no idea, though I know she was severely wounded." the pickpocket said. "She killed the hawk who was keeping an eye on her, so the Lords of the Western Wilderness lost track of her movements. They assumed she died when the sun came up, but she may have been strong enough to survive in daylight."

He crumpled the empty coffee cup.

"Something obviously woke her and Jack Thane is certain she is alive and searching for the Grail. It was the source of her power and she will always desire it."

"And I'm her only link?"

"I fear so. You were in the wrong place at the wrong time." Peazle scratched his cheek awkwardly. Charlie remembered that the boy had also seen the horror of the Gorrodin-Rath, first hand.

"What am I going to do?"

He leant forward on the table, head in his hands. The train was now threading its way through the outskirts of Edinburgh. The centre of the town might be filled with stately Georgian homes, lush parks and magnificent churches, but the suburbs were as grey and industrial as any other city.

"Morgana is controlling the last dark creatures left on earth," Peazle continued, after a while. "She will keep sending them after you, so long as you remain in this world. Your only option is to hide."

They were plunged into darkness as the train roared into the long tunnel that ran under the centre of the city. Charlie and Peazle held their breath and gripped the hand rests of their seats until the leather squeaked. They had no great love of tunnels. When they emerged into daylight, sheer rock rose steeply from the tracks to Edinburgh's magnificent castle, hundreds of feet above. Peazle shivered, remembering he had once been a prisoner there.

"In the meantime, I shall attempt to find Lilly."

Charlie fingered the silver whistle on the chain around his neck. *If you ever really need me, blow this*, the girl had told him, the last time he saw her.

"I know how to do that," he muttered to himself.

A few minutes later, the train pulled slowly into the city's Waverly station.

Sergeant Plune sat at the dining table in the Wilson's kitchen. A tall, bald man with a pockmarked face took off his brown raincoat, entered and introduced himself as Inspector Archer of Birmingham CID.

"I've talked to the parents and no valuables have been taken, not that these people had much to steal. All the rooms were torn apart. Whoever went through them seemed pretty angry and the boy's bedroom was the worst. There's still no sign of him."

"Do the parents have any idea why their house was ransacked?" Plune asked, secretly thrilled to be part of such a big operation.

"They say they haven't a clue," the Inspector replied. "To be honest, they're more worried about where their son might have gone. According to the mum and dad, he's a very sensible lad."

The Inspector looked longingly at the electric kettle, undamaged on the breakfast bar. Plune took the hint and got up to make a cup of tea.

"This one's got me baffled," Inspector Archer admitted. "It's just plain weird. Especially when you take into account that crazy story about some wild cat."

He took Charlie's note, sealed in a plastic bag, from his pocket.

"Then there's this. It seems to indicate the boy left of his own accord." He looked down at his notepad.

"For now, we'll have to treat him as a runaway and start checking local bus and train stations."

He heard a cough from the doorway and turned. Charlie's father was standing there, his expression taught.

"I'm going to look too," he said. "I've been calling his mobile every ten minutes, but there's no answer and the tracker app doesn't seem to work."

"All the more reason to stay put." Inspector Archer put down his mug of tea. "You have to be here in case your son tries to contact you or comes back."

He indicated to a policeman standing in the hall and the uniformed man moved to escort Charlie's dad away.

"Crime scene, you know?" the Inspector said apologetically. Charlie's dad glared at the steaming mug, snorted, and strode off.

"You find any fingerprints?" Sergeant Plume said quietly, and the Inspector nodded.

"All over the place. Mr and Mrs Wilson aren't big on dusting." The Inspector dismissed these potential clues with a shake of his head. "They belong to the occupants. Strange thing is, there are animal hairs all over the house, but the Wilsons say they don't own a pet."

He caught Sergeant Plune's alarmed expression and looked around again. This time Charlie's mother was standing in the doorway. She fixed the Inspector with a steady gaze. Archer was about to rise and usher her out, but the intensity of her stare pinned him to the seat.

Mrs Wilson was very beautiful, he thought, and he noticed her eyes were the deepest, brightest green he had ever seen.

"Find my son, Inspector," she said, her look never wavering.

"I will, ma'am," he said.

"No. Promise me. Promise you'll find him."

Inspector Archer was an experienced investigator and had seen too many missing person cases end in tragedy. He knew no such oath could be kept, so he never made one. He opened his mouth to say something neutral, but the woman's gaze was making the hairs on his neck stand on end. There was more than anguish in that look. There was an intensity that was almost hypnotic.

Even so, Inspector Archer would never understand why he said what he did.

"I promise."

The boys alighted and hurried out of Edinburgh's Waverly station. The sky was beginning to darken and a cold wind whipped at their clothes. Charlie immediately looked to where the Old Town sloped up from the rest of the city, the site of his incredible adventure the previous year. Peazle looked too, taking in the castle, the Gothic steeples and ancient tenements that lined the Old Town ridge, casting serrated shadows over the city. They brought back no fond memories.

"Looks much the same as it did when I saw it last," he grunted. "Two centuries ago."

The streetlights suddenly came on, bathing them in a yellow glow. The pickpocket pulled Charlie back into the shadows, glancing nervously up and down the busy street.

"We have to draw as little attention to ourselves as possible," he hissed in a stage whisper. "Morgana could have eyes anywhere."

"If she does, they'll be blinded by your waistcoat."

"I love this attire," Peazle replied defensively. "But I probably should steal a proper vestment, eh? It's getting a bit chilly."

"Nick a proper hat while you're at it." Charlie fished an apple from his pocket and bit down. He hadn't had a real meal all day and realised he was starving. Being back in Edinburgh, the place where he had already defeated one monster, seemed to have rekindled his spirit of adventure.

"What now?" he said through a mouthful of fruit.

"We need somewhere quiet to lie low till nightfall," he said.

"How about the Underground City?"

"How about I punch you in the snoot?"

"I was joking."

"The great sword Excalibur should still be in Greyfriars graveyard, where you hid it last summer," Peazle said. "We're going to wait until it gets dark properly and dig it up."

"What do we need Excalibur for?"

"It had the power to slay Mordred. I'd like to have it to hand, wouldn't you?"

"Oh yeah. It'll increase your chance of survival from none to just-about-none." Charlie gave a wink. "But I have a little surprise that's going to make our job a lot easier."

Before the pickpocket could stop him, he pulled the silver whistle Lilly had given him from around his neck and blew into it.

There was silence.

"Oh. Maybe it's blocked." The boy held the whistle up to the streetlight and tried to see inside. He put it in his mouth again.

"What are you doing?" Peazle jumped forward and knocked the whistle away. "You want every bobby in the city turning up to see what the commotion is? They won't be able to help us!"

Charlie tried to point out that police didn't use whistles anymore, and he was summoning another type of help entirely, but Peazle grabbed his protesting companion and dragged him away from the station entrance and up the steep hill that led into the Old Town.

Charlie was disappointed. He wanted to see the look of amazement on the Pickpocket's face when Lilly suddenly appeared. Had she lied about helping him?

Peazle was so intent on hurrying them into the anonymity of the Old Town's bustling back streets, neither boy noticed a white hawk with black-tipped wings hovering in the dark sky above. Nor did they see a crouching shape in the deepest shadows of a nearby alley.

If they had, they would have realised that no amount of darkness could disguise the size of its outline.

The figure seemed almost too big to be human.

Greyfriars

There was no point in going into Greyfriars before dark, in case they bumped into sightseers. No one had been buried in the graveyard for over a century, but it was picturesque and historic, so people often visited during the day. The boys went instead to the City Restaurant, an upmarket fish and chip shop with chrome fittings and red leather seats. Charlie ordered dinner and Peazle took off his coat - a fur-lined parka that he had 'borrowed' from a washing line behind one of the Old Town tenements. The waitress politely ignored his multicoloured waistcoat. Halfway through the meal, the pickpocket sat back and folded his hands contentedly over his stomach.

"If I'd lived and died in the 19th century, like all the other people I knew, I'd never have tasted fish in batter or Cokey Cola. Life just isn't fair, sometimes."

"Tell me about it," said Charlie sourly.

"Ach, you're lucky in many ways. You live in a world of scientific advancements, the people in my time couldn't have dreamt of." The pickpocket was unable to contain his passion. "Have you ever used an electric toothbrush?"

"How do you know about stuff in my world, if you live in Galhadria?"

"Jack Thane sends me here, now and then - though not nearly often enough. I always have to come straight back or face his wrath." Peazle got a second wind and shovelled another huge forkful of mushy peas into his mouth. "Pass me some more of that... tomato sauce is it called? Wondrous stuff."

"How do you get back and forward?"

"Thin Places, of course. They're few and far between, but I have a map."

"Why exactly does Jack Thane send you on trips to earth?"

"You think I'm a spy, Charlie?"

"Just curious." The boy nibbled at a chip. "Listen, Peazle, I appreciate this Thane guy has a lot of confidence in you - sending a thirteen-year-old boy to save me from a rampaging monster.

"I've lived two centuries, by the way, but your sarcasm is noted."

"But why aren't the Lords of the Western Wilderness helping you?"

"Magical creatures do not...."

"Magical creatures do not fight magical creatures, I know!" Charlie waved a handful of chips at the pickpocket, who tried to ward off flying ketchup. "But WHY?"

"The Little People don't talk about it," Peazle said, leaning forward. "But I'm small and folk tend not to notice me. I hear things I'm not supposed to. Plus I love to study. The Lords have a great library and I find things there."

"Like what?"

"Long ago in Galhadria," Peazle leaned even closer. "There was a terrible civil war. When it was finally over, the greatest sorcerers of the land plotted to make sure it would never happen again."

"The Lords of the Western Wilderness?"

"The very same," the pickpocket replied. "Gorrodin was one, at that time. Together they wove a great enchantment. I'm not sure the exact details, but it worked something like this... Should two magical forces ever take sides against each other again, whichever side struck the first deadly blow would ultimately lose."

Peazle laughed cynically.

"It was called the Dolorous Stroke and the Lords thought the threat of it enough to guarantee peace forever."

"Magical creature must not fight magical creature - the rule no Galhadrian can break." Charlie nodded. "That's where it comes from."

"It does. It is ingrained in their culture."

"All right, I can see that." Charlie conceded. "But it doesn't explain why the Galhadrians are determined to stay hidden from us humans. We're not magical."

"The Lords have powers you couldn't imagine," Peazle pointed to a small TV, high on a bracket behind the café counter. The sound was off, but Charlie could see armed soldiers in Khaki surveying the aftermath of a bomb blast in some Middle Eastern country. A bleeding child was being pulled, crying, from the wreckage of a burning car.

"Men have immense power too, Charlie. It's called science. And that power is growing faster than you can control." Peazle looked sadly at his dinner companion.

"They're afraid of us."

The pickpocket pulled a fob watch from inside his waistcoat and looked at it.

"The graveyard should be deserted by now." He stood and put on his coat. "Let's get the sword."

It was Saturday night, and the streets of the Old Town were filled with revellers out enjoying themselves. Nobody paid much attention to the two boys, especially since Peazle's new parka covered his outlandish waistcoat and the hood partly obscured his bowler hat. The pair finally reached the gates of the walled graveyard, set back from the houses, lit dimly by one distant streetlight.

They were closed.

"That's just great," moaned Charlie. "Somebody must have started locking it at night."

"All the better." Peazle stepped up to the gate, pulled a small cloth bundle from his pocket and removed a sliver of metal.

"Sometimes, I think I chose the right profession after all." He bent over and, a few seconds later, there was a click and the gate slowly swung open.

"Two hundred years may have passed, but basic lock design is still the same." He ushered Charlie into the graveyard and secured the gates again.

The boys moved cautiously between the gravestones, hands stretched in front of them, trying to get accustomed to the dark. They skirted the black mass of Greyfriars church and crept through the inky shadows until they reached the area where the poet, James Hogg, was buried. Eight months ago, Charlie had concealed Excalibur at that very spot.

"How are we going to dig the sword out?" hissed Charlie. "I can't see a bloody thing."

"You think I wouldn't come prepared?" Peazle trotted over to one of the nearby mausoleums, a solid block of darkness resting against the graveyard wall. There were several clinking sounds and the iron door of the upright tomb swung open as easily as the cemetery gate had. Moments later, a torch beam cut across the distance between them.

"Greyfriars is a Thin Place, remember?" the pickpocket's voice floated gleefully from behind the beam. Seconds later, he was back, carrying two torches and a shovel. "I planted these in that mausoleum a couple of days ago. I would have dug up Excalibur myself, only you seem to be the only person that can pull it from the ground. It seems to have bonded with you."

He shone the torch beam into his own face and Charlie saw his curious expression.

"Why do you suppose that is?"

"I haven't got a clue." Charlie took the spade and plunged it into the earth behind James Hogg's headstone. Peazle lit up the spot so the boy could see where he was digging.

"Me neither. And if the Lords of the Western Wilderness know, they haven't told me." The pickpocket sounded faintly annoyed.

Metal clinked against something solid and Peazle bent closer, directing the flashlight beam into the hole. The hilt of a sword protruded from the soil. Charlie grabbed it, pulled, and Excalibur slid easily out of the ground.

"This might be a bad time to bring it up." The boy held the gleaming sword in the air. "But I'm not going to Galhadria. I'm coming with you to find Lilly."

Instead of objecting, Peazle motioned for silence, listening carefully.

"Shhhhhhh. Do you hear something?"

"Don't be freaking me out, bro."

"I heard the gate rattling."

"Then let's get out of here. Could we use the Thin Place, after all, but come out somewhere else?"

"I'm not opening a Thin Place if a bunch of drunken teenagers are about to come staggering around the corner."

"What if it's Morgana that comes round the corner?" Charlie hissed. But Peazle had snapped off the flashlight and was already moving away, crouching low to the ground. Charlie sighed and followed him, scurrying after the dark, bobbing shape.

They rounded the corner of the church. A full moon floated just above the sharp points of the closed cemetery gates, its pale light bleeding down onto the empty path. There was no sign of any intruders. Peazle stopped and straightened up.

"Perhaps I am being a little over-cautious," he began. "What's the matter?"

Charlie was staring in horror at the pickpocket. Or rather, what was behind him. A huge shape was rising above the nearest gravestone, moonlight silhouetting its hulking form. Two massive arms arched over the top of the tomb, reaching out for the boy.

"Peazle! Get down!" Charlie shouted, leaping forward. The pickpocket's childhood instinct for survival kicked in and he threw himself to the ground. Charlie leapt onto his friend's back and used the leverage to propel himself high into the air, swinging his sword as he went.

Inches from the creature's massive head, Excalibur's silver blade clashed against another sword, as a second figure shot up behind the gravestone. Sparks flew from the clashing weapons, the monster fell backwards with a yelp and Charlie went somersaulting over it, landing awkwardly on his side. In a second, he was on his feet again, weapon held in front of him.

"My compliments!" The swordsman facing him was a tall youth with long dark hair. "You handle that weapon as if ye were born with one in your hand."

The boy spoke in a thick northern accent, one that Charlie remembered from their brief meeting eight months ago. Peazle rose to his feet, grinning.

"Duncan?" He shouted gleefully. "Is that you?"

"It is indeed." Duncan sheathed his sword and shook the pickpocket's hand. "Your wee pal almost took the head off Shadowjack here."

The enormous figure sat up, shaking its head. A toothy smile split the darkness.

"Is this all the thanks I get for keeping an eye on you two all night?" Shadowjack Henry laughed.

The Worms

The introductions were brief. Charlie sheepishly shook hands with Duncan and stared at Shadowjack. He had never seen a man as large as the blacksmith.

"What are you two doing here?" the pickpocket beamed.

"Jack Thane came calling," Duncan said. "He asked if we'd help you escort this boy tae safety." The highlander indicated Charlie. "And perhaps fight a monster or two. Sounded simple enough."

"After all that time in Galhadria, I was dying for a change," Shadowjack added.

"We've been following since you arrived in Edinburgh, tae make sure none of Morgana's agents were right behind. Nae sign of any trouble, though." The highlander sounded a little disappointed. "So what now? Back through the Thin Place and nae real adventure?"

"I, for one, am keen to get out of Greyfriars." Shadowjack Henry looked longingly towards the cemetery entrance. "Something bad always seems to happen here."

"Shadowjack?" Charlie looked up at the ugly iron tips of the barrier. "How did you get in?"

"Young Peazle here must have picked the lock," re-plied Shadowjack, patting the boy on the shoulder so hard the pickpocket's knees buckled.

"That I did," Peazle said warily. "I also secured it behind me."

Duncan looked sharply round.

"It was open a minute ago," Shadowjack looked bewildered. "I strolled right in."

The highlander's sword slid from its scabbard and glistened in the moonlight. The cemetery was ringed by a fifteen-foot stone wall - even a giant like Shadowjack couldn't scale it – and the gates were the only way in or out. The highlander cursed himself silently for not spotting the obvious.

Greyfriars Graveyard was the perfect place for an ambush.

"Damn!" Duncan hissed. "This is a trap!"

And he turned and sprinted towards the Thin Place.

"Go!" shouted Shadowjack pushing Peazle in front of him. "Little man. That torch, throw it here! You and the highlander, on our flanks!"

Charlie tossed his flashlight to the blacksmith. Duncan was on the right of the group, sword in hand, so Charlie moved to the left, brandishing Excalibur as he ran. The group dashed across the graveyard in silence, leaping over tombstones, the torch beam bobbing in the darkness. Peazle pulled a notebook from his parka pocket as he fled and vainly tried to shine his wavering light on it.

"I've got the incantation for opening the gateway to Galhadria written down," he panted.

"You didn't memorise it!?"

"It's about nine yards long!"

"The Thin Place is straight ahead," Duncan said, clearing a high gravestone with an effortless hop. "Better get incanting."

"Wait!" He skidded to a halt, holding his sword to the side to stop his comrades' advance.

"Make up your mind!"

"Shine your lights on the ground."

Shadowjack and Peazle did so.

"What foul magic is this?" Shadowjack breathed.

The earth in front of Hogg's grave seemed to be coming alive, seething and writhing, as if the bodies buried underneath were trying to break free. The party watched in horror as twigs, bones and rocks breached the churning, broken soil. Then worms began to boil to the surface. Thousands upon thousands of them.

"Back! We have to go back!" Peazle whirled and shone the light the way they had come. But the soil behind them was erupting too.

"We'll be swallowed by the earth!" he wailed.

Duncan scanned the graveyard, refusing to panic.

"Into that tree," he pointed. A thick oak twisted out of the ground, next to the graveyard wall, less than twenty yards away, the branches curving over the top of the barrier and into the darkness. Without looking backwards, the highlander slammed his sword into the scabbard on his back and darted to the tree. He climbed swiftly, uttering only a few quiet grunts and was soon scrambling through the middle branches. Seconds later, Shadowjack, Peazle and Charlie were clawing their way up the trunk behind him, ignoring the rough bark that tore their elbows and knees.

"Watch what you're doing with Excalibur," Peazle squealed. "You almost had my eye out."

"I'm trying to hurry you up."

"Tell the big lump in front of me!"

"Another few feet and these branches won't hold my weight," Shadowjack shouted, accompanied by cracking and breaking sounds, as he tried to force his way through the intertwining limbs. His foot hit Peazle in the head and the pickpocket dropped the flashlight. Charlie looked down as it hit the ground.

The base of the tree looked to be anchored in a stormy brown sea and a gap was appearing at its base, as the earth sucked into itself, like sand in an hourglass. The torch sank into the widening hole and vanished.

"Climb higher!" Charlie screamed. "They're trying to bring the tree down!"

Shadowjack and Peazle were fighting their way through the middle of the foliage, Peazle wriggling through the branches like an eel, while Shadowjack simply hauled the limbs out of their supporting wood and tossed them away. Duncan had reached a stout overhanging branch and was edging his way along it.

A few more feet and he would be able to touch the top of the graveyard wall.

"We're almost there!" the highlander yelled encouragingly.

The oak gave a tortured groan and lurched back a few feet. Duncan yelped and slipped from his perch. He grabbed a branch as he fell and managed to hang on, swinging by one arm, his face a tight mask of pain. Below him, a great gap opened in the earth, a monstrous black mouth.

Then the oak was falling and Charlie realised the trunk he was clinging to would crush him when it hit the ground. A tall, angel-topped monument rose up on one side and he vaulted sideways towards it, thrusting Excalibur in front of him. The sword slid into the stone and Charlie's breath was slammed out of his body as he hit the monument. But he kept hold of Excalibur, feet scrambling for footholds on the smooth marble. There were none and, suddenly, he was hanging just above the boiling earth, both hands clutching the hilt of the sword. He silently thanked his parents for teaching him their acrobatic skills.

The oak hit the earth with a mighty crash. From the centre of the branches, Shadowjack's torch beam still wobbled and spun as he, Duncan and Peazle clawed their way through the broken foliage and back onto the trunk. All around the toppled tree, the earth frothed and jumped, as millions of worms seethed and chewed at the bark, trying to reach the stranded humans. To

Charlie's dismay, he realised both his gravestone and the fallen tree were beginning to sink into the churning mud. The monument gave a sudden drop and he almost lost his handhold. Burning bile rose in his throat.

"Please God, I don't want to die like this," he cried softly to himself.

As he prayed, a shaft of light cut across the graveyard. Not the weak beam of a torch - but a shimmering beacon. Charlie twisted his head to see where it was coming from.

A tiny figure stood, far away, at the gates of the cemetery - bathed in brilliant luminescence. It raised one hand, made a fist, and brought it down forcefully. Every tombstone in the graveyard, between the stranded party and the gates, fell flat with a dull thump and a blast of cold air swept through Charlie's hair.

There was a shout of triumph to his right as Duncan leapt off the sinking trunk. He landed on a flat gravestone, shaking an army of worms from his boots in disgust.

"This is our way oot!" he shouted. "But they'll no stay above ground for long."

Then he was off, leaping from flattened tombstone to flattened tombstone. The others did not need any prompting. Charlie hauled Excalibur free and launched himself into space. He landed on his back and saw stars. Within seconds, worms were swarming over his arms and legs, pawing at him like a million squirming fingers. With a moan of revulsion, he tried to roll towards the closest toppled gravestone. He put one arm out and it sank into the earth, up to his shoulder. Slimy, wriggling bodies surged over his face and he pulled back his arm, hidden by a mass of quivering worms. He thrust Excalibur in front of him and the earth itself seemed to recoil from the Great Sword. Scything the weapon back and forth, he groped the last few feet and flopped onto the cold stone. Turning his head sideways, he caught a glimpse of his companions fighting for their lives.

Peazle had jumped off the tree, only to sink up to his waist in churning grubs and worms. Now he was screaming in terror, arms raised above his head. As he slid into the earth, Shadowjack came thundering past. Reaching out one mighty arm, he grabbed the shrieking pickpocket by the hair and pulled with all his might. With a wail that put his earlier efforts to shame, Peazle shot out of the ground. Shadowjack stuck him under a beefy arm and began hopping from one tombstone to another, zigzagging towards the gate.

Charlie's tombstone was now being lapped by an ocean of squirming pink flesh. It dropped a few inches, then the boy was leaping from gravestone to gravestone, trying not to slip on squashed, oily bodies, heading towards the exit. He reached the safety of the concrete driveway, right behind the others and collapsed in a heap. Beside him lay Peazle, Duncan and Shadowjack, all pulling worms from their clothing and hair and gasping with relief.

The bright light had gone and only the faint yellow illumination of the street light allowed them to see when the last of the twisting pink bodies had gone.

A small figure stepped from the shadows.

"Did someone whistle?" The voice was weak with exhaustion but Charlie recognised it immediately. He rolled onto his stomach and looked up.

"Nice timing, Lilly," he said

"Fashionably late." The girl gave a small smile and nodded politely. She turned to the highlander.

"Hi there, Duncan."

"Hello again, Heather. I mean, eh... Lilly."

"Whatever you're called, I thank you from the bottom of my heart, lass." Shadowjack got up, bowed, then pulled a last fat worm from his beard. "Before we make more formal introductions, is there anywhere I could have a bath?"

"We tried tae lodge at an inn earlier," Duncan said sheepishly. "But Shadowjack got stuck in something called a revolving door."

"I'd never been in a fancy hotel before," Shadowjack said proudly.

"I can take us to lodgings." Lilly stepped out into the street, looked around and beckoned for the others to follow.

"Stay in the shadows, though. You look as if you've crawled out of your own graves."

An hour later, Jack Thane stood among the ruins of Greyfriars Graveyard. Lord Math was beside him - a black velvet cloak protecting her from the cold. Beyond them, a third shadowy figure crouched behind a gravestone, sniffing the ground. All three were bathed in the pale blue glow of the Thin Place, shining in the air like an upright pool. It also lit up the flattened headstones and fallen trees.

"They did not make it to Galhadria, Thane," Math said smugly.

"Charlie Wilson's whistle summoned Lilly, as he hoped," Thane replied. "Regretfully, it also alerted Morgana as to their exact whereabouts."

Thane knelt and studied the ground. "It's possible they will try to get through the Thin Place tomorrow."

"Would you?" Math grunted sceptically, looking at the broken headstones surrounded by a sea of dead worms - the earth, an expanse of flayed brown skin, turned inside out. "The worms will still be here and the area crawling with humans too, I'll wager."

"Perhaps that is for the best." The wizard gave a sly smile. "Peazle is no fool and that is why I sent him. He has persuaded the Wilson boy to come north and now he has found Lilly. I imagine they will search for the cup itself, rather than immediately retreating to Galhadria."

Math sniffed.

"Does the awakening of one long vanished creature really warrant all this... excitement?"

"Have you no eyes?" Jack Thane snapped, sweeping his arm across the devastation. "Look at this."

He dipped his fingers into the ruined earth and lifted a dirty clod, thick with dead worms.

"Morgana should not have this kind of power."

"True." His companion frowned. "But she does. In which case, do you really think the boy and his companions can stay alive, long enough to make it back?"

"As you can see, they are not food for the worms yet." Thane shrugged. "But you are right. I do not see how they could possibly succeed."

Jack Thane stood, releasing the handful of soil as he rose.

"No matter. If Lilly knows where the Grail is, she would not reveal it to us, for we have treated her badly. But she may show its whereabouts to the Wilson child and I will be watching."

"If their quest is so important, perhaps we *should* act to help."

"The rest of the Lords will not agree to our interfering on earth, as you know. By the time we convince them Morgana is as great a threat to us as she is to mankind, it will be too late."

He snapped his fingers at the creature behind the tombstone. The Cat Palug stepped into the light, glaring at him with baleful yellow eyes.

"I have started the Wilson boy running." The Lord gave a rueful smile. "He has led Peazle to Lilly, as I hoped. Let us also hope they retrieve the Grail and reach another thin place before Morgana's forces catch up with them."

"Are you so sure the girl knows where it is?"

"I am not." Jack Thane attached a leather leash around the creature's neck and straightened up.

"But she is our best bet and, as I say, I shall be watching."

With a gentlemanly bow, he took Math's arm and, as if they were going for a moonlight stroll, the Galhadrians stepped through the Thin Place and vanished.

Part 2

'In Scotland, the Templars, specifically the St Clairs, were the guardians of holy relics… one suggestion is that the Grail Cup is hidden in the St Clairs' Rosslyn Chapel, near Edinburgh.'

Cassandra Eason. *The Encyclopaedia of Magic & Ancient Wisdom.*

Hotel Huntingdon

The night brought a strange mixture of joy and sorrow. At first, the very fact they were alive had been cause for celebration. Lilly took the others to a nearby hotel - the Huntingdon - tall, modern and expensive. The bedraggled party tripped pensively into a huge black and white tiled lobby and tried to look inconspicuous behind a group of spiky potted plants, though Shadowjack would have had as much success if he had been hiding behind a twig. Lilly walked briskly over to the reception desk, where the counter staff were whispering suspiciously to each other. She waved her hands a few times and the blazer clad receptionists suddenly looked blank, as if they weren't quite sure who they were. A few minutes later, Lilly, Peazle, Duncan, Shadowjack and Charlie found themselves on the top floor, being escorted to the Penthouse Suite by an equally bemused porter.

"I must learn how to do this magic stuff," Charlie said, racing around the huge suite, opening and closing every door he could find. "This cupboard is bigger than my whole house."

While the rest explored their plush surroundings, Lilly announced she was going to find fresh clothes and food. While she was gone, the others took turns to clean up in the huge white bathroom. Shadowjack was unimpressed by the invention of the shower.

"It's just a wee hose sticking out of the wall," he shouted. "What happens if I turn this red lever here? Yeeeeeaaaaaaaaaaaah!"

Lilly staggered back in laden with plastic bags advertising the hotel shop.

"How did you persuade reception to open the store at one in the morning?"

"I made them think it was one in the afternoon." She upended the bulging bags and provisions and clothes tumbled out onto the floor. Charlie noticed that the girl had dark circles under her eyes. True, it was late, but it occurred to the boy that he had never really seen Lilly perform this much magic before. It seemed to require immense effort on her part.

Soon they were all lounging on the thick white carpet, drinking Coke and eating crisps. Each of the boys now wore jeans and woolly jumpers, though Peazle still had on his bowler hat and Duncan had wrapped the tartan plaid around his waist

"I don't suppose you could swap this for one in plum?" Shadowjack inquired, tugging his sweater.

"Think yourself lucky," Lilly sniffed. "When I told the staff your chest size, they thought it was a joke."

Now that they were all comfortable, Peazle introduced Shadowjack and Duncan formally to Charlie and everyone thanked Lilly again for saving their lives.

"I came when I heard Charlie's whistle, just as I promised," said the girl matter-of-factly. "I didn't expect to be called so soon, or to find all of you with him." She looked around the assembled group with a raised eyebrow. "Just what is going on?"

"A simple errand, lass," Shadowjack emptied an entire packet of prawn cocktail crisps into his mouth. "We've to find some goblet and bring it back to Galhadria."

The girl frowned, as if something were scratching at the edges of her memory. Charlie nudged Peazle.

"You've still got some of that potion you gave me, don't you?" he whispered.

The pickpocket nodded.

"What would happen if you gave it to Lilly?"

The pickpocket's eyes widened and he got quickly to his feet.

"Would you accompany me to the balcony, Lilly?" he said, holding out his hand. His voice sounded casual, but the tips of his fingers trembled. "There are a few things I… eh… need to show you, and you might appreciate some privacy."

Before the girl could protest, he took her gently by the arm and led her away.

Duncan and Shadowjack looked at Charlie, puzzled.

"What was all that about?" said the giant, opening another packet of crisps.

"Lilly's about to find out some rather horrible things," Charlie said flatly.

"Like what?"

"It's hard to know where to start." He held up one hand and ticked off facts. "One. For fifteen hundred years, she thought her father was a traitor. Turns out he was actually a hero. Two. The Lords of the Western Wilderness could have set her straight and didn't. Three. Her mother is the monster who's chasing me and almost killed us tonight."

There was silence for a long time. Duncan's face darkened and he bowed his head. Shadowjack stared into his empty crisp packet, his bushy brows knitted together.

"Poor wee lassie," he said eventually.

Peazle came back in, shutting the balcony door behind him.

"That was quick." Charlie looked up, surprised.

The pickpocket bowed his head.

"She remembers everything," he said quietly.

Charlie and Duncan began to rise, but Peazle stopped them.

"She wants to be left alone," he said, shaking his head. "Said she'll see you in the morning."

"And what then?"

"I don't know." The pickpocket flopped down on one of the beds. "She may know where the Grail is. It didn't seem the right time to ask."

For a while, the four talked softly to each other, though, every now and then, one or the other cast a glance at the patio door leading to the balcony. But the door was smoked glass and it was dark outside. They could not see Lilly.

Peazle, Shadowjack and Duncan caught up with the last hundred years. Though they had been friends on earth, they had gone their separate ways in Galhadria. In a land without telephones or emails, the three companions soon lost touch completely.

Shadowjack had set up his forge on a rolling green meadow and become an expert at working faerie metals into jewellery. His work was much prized by the Galhadrians. Peazle had spent his time studying art and science. The Lords of the Western Wilderness kept an extensive library in their great stronghold of Castle Alclud, on the edge of Galhadria. In return for access to their books, the pickpocket was sent on 'errands' such as the one he was engaged in now.

"That's a lot of work just to get a library card," Charlie said sarcastically.

Duncan told how he had travelled the length and breadth of Galhadria, looking for his missing brother, taken as a baby two hundred years ago. Highland lore was full of tales about how the Little People used to steal human children. Though the Galhadrians swore these were nonsense, the highlander still searched. He had never found him.

Charlie related his adventures and explained why he had to leave his parents. The others instinctively looked towards the balcony again.

Eventually, the conversation drifted to more mundane matters. Duncan couldn't believe that a kilt now cost £400 and looked like a skirt and Shadowjack wanted to know what a prawn was. And there they lay, on the soft, deep carpet, talking and slowly getting to know each other again until, one by one, they drifted off to sleep.

All but one.

The Balcony

A bank of heavy purple cloud crawled sluggishly across the night sky, bruised by the spires and tenements of Edinburgh. The smoked glass door slid quietly open and Duncan stepped out onto the hotel balcony. A gust of wind arched around the side of the building and tugged at his unruly locks. Lilly was perched, like a small green bird. on the stone parapet that bordered the balcony, staring sightlessly into the night. Duncan walked softly over and peered into the street. A car horn honked intrusively in the darkness.

"Sixteen hundred years," Lilly said. "All that time, I believed my father had deserted me."

"Aye. And now you know he didnae." Duncan spread his hands. "Better you were wrong for a thousand years than right about your paw being a traitor."

"He's been trapped all this time and I never tried to rescue him." Tears glittered in the girl's eyes. "I deserted him!"

"A spell was put upon you, Lilly." Duncan put out his arm and touched her shoulder. It was cold as the night wind. "You must find your father and explain that. You say he is a great wizard. He, of all people, should understand."

"He'll understand the Lords of the Western Wilderness left both of us to rot. His anger will be great."

Lilly shivered. The highlander climbed onto the parapet and crouched beside her small figure. Together they watched the red tail lights of cars gliding past, a hundred feet below. On top of the ledge the wind was stronger, and the tartan plaid snapped and fluttered in the breeze. Lilly saw that the boy's sword was still fastened to his back. Duncan noticed her glance.

"It doesnae feel right unless I'm wearing it," he said simply.

"That's a shame."

The highlander nodded and draped the plaid back over his weapon.

"I have spent two hundred years looking for my missing brother, without success," he said, finally. He looked up at the few stars, visible through angry clouds and ran a hand wearily through his hair. "That's no nearly as long as you've been apart from your kin."

Lilly looked sideways at the highlander, his hair blowing in the wind, dark as a raven's wing.

"To the Devil with Jack Thane and his orders," he said. "I will go with you if you wish to free your father. You have my word."

With a grunt, he hopped down from the ledge and held out his hand. The girl hesitated, then smiled and allowed him to escort her from the perch. She stood behind the highlander, using him as shelter from the biting wind. Duncan had forgotten how small she was.

"You look younger than I remember," the highlander said. "But I know that's because I am older."

He smiled at her briefly, though smiling no longer seemed natural to his face.

"I remember you as Heather, the Gypsy who captured my heart and saved my life." He unwrapped the plaid from around his waist and draped it over her shoulders. "But she is gone. Now you are Lilly - a lassie who needs her father."

He bowed stiffly.

"Half Galhadrian you may be, and God knows I have nae great love for your race - but I am at your service."

Lilly darted forward and kissed him on the cheek while his head was at her level. Duncan stood up, surprised and pleased. Lilly bowed in turn.

"I gratefully accept your help, highlander."

The balcony door slid open and Duncan's hand automatically went to his sword. Peazle stood in the entrance, bowler hat in his hand, fingers drumming nervously on the brim.

"May I intrude?" he asked.

"You were listening behind the door?" Duncan's eyes narrowed in irritation.

"Old habits die hard." The pickpocket turned and faced Lilly. "I understand that you want to rescue your father, but we have to get you to safety. You have shown yourself and now Morgana will be after you."

"Yes. And you led her straight to me." Lilly looked the pickpocket in the eye.

"I'm sorry for that." Peazle straightened his shoulders and stared back defiantly. "But it's all the more reason why you should seek refuge in Galhadria. I, however, have been tasked with finding the Grail Cup. If you know where it is, tell me and I will endeavour to retrieve it before Morgana."

"I have a better suggestion." The voice came from behind them. They turned to see Charlie standing a few feet away, just inside the sliding door.

"Why don't we find the Grail ourselves, then take it to its rightful owner?" He stepped forward. "We can free Lilly's father and give him back his talisman."

"The Lords of the Western Wilderness have their flaws, granted." Peazle slapped his hat in exasperation. "But they are powerful sorcerers and can protect us from Morgana."

"So could my father if he had his cup back," Lilly protested.

"Are you sure?" Peazle asked. "He once loved your mother, remember?"

"So did I." Lilly's voice was cold.

"The more I hear about these Lords of the Western Wilderness, the less I trust them." Charlie broke in. "I say we find the Grail, take it to Gorrodin, and ask for his help instead."

A shadow fell across Charlie as Shadowjack Henry moved into the doorway behind him. He gave Lilly a bristling smile.

"What is this?" Peazle sighed in exasperation. "A party?"

"You have saved my life twice now, wee lass, once from Mordred and once from Morgana." The blacksmith stepped onto the balcony, moved Peazle and Charlie gently aside, then bent on one knee before the girl. "I, too, will help you find the Grail and return it to your father."

"Listen, old friend." Duncan placed his hand on the pickpocket's shoulder. "Jack Thane has sent you on a bad errand. Away back and tell him that his underlings have mutinied. He'll not blame you."

Peazle shook his head and a slow, unexpected smile split the boy's face.

"Why tip him off at all?" he said mischievously. "As long as I stay with you, Jack Thane will assume we're still trying to get back to Galhadria through another thin place. After all, Greyfriars is hardly safe."

He stuck the bowler back on his head and set it at a jaunty angle.

"I can't let you go on an adventure like this without me. You'd never make it."

Duncan smiled a genuine smile for the first time since returning to his old home.

"Then we are a Clan," he announced proudly. "Our loyalty is to each other."

"If that's settled, can we please get some sleep?" Shadowjack Henry yawned. "Tomorrow, we have to search for this blessed Grail with God knows what chasing us." He turned hopefully back to Lilly.

"Unless you know where your father's cup is."

"I have absolutely no idea," she said. Then she gave a dainty smile.

"But I know someone who does."

Hunting Charlie Wilson

Charlie and his companions woke early, with a new sense of purpose. They would find the Grail and free Lilly's father. With his help, they would defeat Morgana and be free to do what they wished afterwards. Of course, Morgana looked to be a formidable enemy, and each secretly worried what the Lords would do about this deception - but they were comforted by the fact that they were together. It seemed right somehow.

"As you say, highlander, we are our own wee Clan." Shadowjack Henry stretched and rubbed his bushy black beard. "We stick together, no matter what may befall us."

Duncan smiled to himself as he pulled the new jumper over his head. Even Lilly seemed cheerful - relieved to know the truth, more than angry at what had happened to her. Charlie supposed her Galhadrian half allowed the girl to shrug off such shattering misfortune. And she was obviously delighted at the idea of being reunited with her father.

"So, where do we start?" Duncan asked as they packed their belongings. Lilly had made a morning trip to the shops and brought back sleeping bags, tents and rucksacks. The highlander was eager to be off and looking. He considered himself rather an expert at searching.

"I gave my father's talisman to one of Arthur's men - a warrior named Uallabh. He promised to meet me at the Glen of Rosslyn." Lilly picked up Excalibur and slid it into a long plastic tube used to hold fishing rods. Duncan did the same with his own sword, smiling with approval at how well this disguised the weapons.

"When was this?" Shadowjack asked, fastening his rucksack.

"I'm not sure. Sometime in the early 7th century?"

The rest stopped packing and stared at her.

"He won't be dead," she protested. "He drank from the cup. He's immortal now." She paused and gave a worried shrug. "If he didn't try to use the powers the Grail gave him… he's eh…. probably still human."

Shadowjack snorted and gave the strap of his rucksack a mighty tug. It snapped off in his hand.

"Shoddy workmanship they have these days," he grumbled, reading the label on the pack. "What is Taiwan anyway?"

"Lilly," Charlie said tentatively. "What makes you think he'll still be waiting, after thirteen centuries? I'd have got a bit fed up by now. You know. Maybe figured that you weren't actually coming."

"He was one of Arthur's greatest warriors." Lilly gave him a disapproving look. "He gave his word."

Charlie, wisely, kept quiet. Peazle looked up from a map he had been studying.

"There's a village called Rosslyn about twenty miles from here. It has an ancient chapel overlooking a glen. That the place?"

"Sounds like it." Duncan shouldered his rucksack and picked up his fishing tube. "Can you magic us there?"

"Not a chance." Lilly gave a sigh. "I may be the daughter of a great sorcerer but I have no talisman of my own and I'm only half Galhadrian. That little trick in the graveyard last night took all my strength – and it was just tipping over a few headstones."

Duncan accepted this stoically.

"How long will it take to walk?"

"No need," Peazle grinned, folding the map and tucking it inside his shirt. "There's a wonderful new invention called the autobus. You'll love it."

Charlie's party trooped out of the elevator and through the hotel foyer. Lilly blew the morning staff a kiss as she waltzed out of the door and into the sunshine. Puzzled by the appearance of such an odd-looking party, the staff looked up the hotel register. There was no record of anyone booking in the night before.

Inspector Archer sat alone at his desk. His tiny office was painted a dull olive and filled with cheap metal furniture. In the corner were overflowing boxes of files, along with a kettle, a bag of sugar and some dirty cups. A small television hooked to an ancient video machine crackled in one corner of the room, playing footage taken by a CCTV camera mounted at Birmingham's central train station. In his hand, the policeman held the statement made by Gary Macmillan. It was short and to the point for Macmillan wasn't keen on talking to the police, at the best of times, especially when it involved describing an attack by a cat with hands. Already he was a laughing stock at school, a situation he found necessary to rectify by using his fists.

The Inspector wasn't interested in some cock-and-bull story about a mutant cat. But he was very interested in the bully's insistence that Charlie Wilson had run off with a boy wearing a bowler hat and bright yellow waistcoat.

Archer yawned, stretched then glanced at the TV once more. The yawn froze on his face. The footage was jumpy and grainy but there was no mistaking what he was watching.

Two young boys, one wearing a bowler hat, were crossing the screen, heading for the train due to leave for Edinburgh. The Inspector looked down at the photograph Mrs Wilson had given him of their son. It was hard to see the other boy's face but the Inspector was in no doubt who his companion was.

Charlie Wilson.

The Clan piled onto the bus for Rosslyn and Shadowjack and Duncan made straight for the back seat. Both sat with their noses pressed against the grimy brown windows, watching the wonders of the world roll past.

"Hey Charlie," the highlander said, pointing into the air. "Why is that wee bird flying so slowly?"

"It's a plane." Charlie glanced up. "It's far away. People fly inside them all over the world."

"Aye, right. And my Uncle Fraser became the Queen of Sheba."

Shadowjack's seat squeaked and strained as he squirmed around, trying to see out of all four windows at once.

"What an amazing place the world is now!" he marvelled, a grin splitting his bristling beard. "What great happiness such marvels must bring. I'll wager there's no more famine or disease or war."

Charlie and Lilly looked at each other.

"There are no more blacksmiths, that's for sure." Peazle looked up from the *Guide to Scotland* he had stolen in the bus station. Shadowjack gave a dismissive snort.

"I don't care. After this is over, I'm learning to be a bus driver."

"What have you found?" Charlie looked at the book over Peazle's shoulder.

"There's a castle and a chapel at Rosslyn Glen." He read. "They were built in the 15th century. The castle's just a ruin now but the chapel is still intact. Famous for the ornate carvings inside… eh… what else?"

Peazle tried to hold the book steady, as the bus rattled out of Edinburgh and into the countryside.

"The chapel was the headquarters of the Knights Templar... I read about them in the library at Galhadria... they were an order of ancient knights dedicated to doing good." He looked around to make sure everybody appreciated his breadth of knowledge, but Shadowjack and Duncan were waving to cars through the back window and Lilly had fallen asleep.

"I'm listening," Charlie said apologetically.

"Hmmm. According to legend, the Knights Templar were alleged to have used the chapel as a hiding place for..." the pickpocket looked up at Charlie, tapping the book nervously.

"A hiding place for what?"

"The Holy Grail."

Charlie sat back, blinking rapidly.

"Holy smoke."

"You don't think?"

Charlie smiled thoughtfully.

"Lilly once told me that all legends get twisted over the course of time." He spoke quietly so as not to wake the sleeping girl. "But they always have a grain of truth at the core."

"I can see where this legend might come from." The pickpocket held up the open guidebook. "Lilly gives her father's magical cup, called the Grail, to one of Arthur's warriors and arranges to meet him at a valley called Rosslyn." He winked. "Now there's a chapel in the same place, that's supposed to be the hiding place for surprise, surprise… a magical cup called the Grail. Our mysterious warrior will surely be long gone, but he was certainly around at one time."

Peazle shut the book with a snap, and Lilly opened her eyes.

"Are we there yet?" she yawned.

"No," Charlie smiled, patting her arm. "But we're an awful lot closer than we were."

Rosslyn

Rosslyn chapel was half a mile from the village of the same name - a small building with graceful stone buttresses and arches that seemed ornate as lace. It sat on the edge of Rosslyn Glen - a precipitous and heavily wooded gorge, with an expanse of level farmland behind it. Swathes of bulging greenery locked together to hide the valley floor, but the Clan could hear the hiss of a river churning, far below the thick canopy.

Duncan immediately placed himself outside the chapel door, the best place to keep watch for anyone following them. Shadowjack had bought a disposable camera in the gift shop and wanted to try taking pictures of the view. Peazle sat in the church garden under a weeping willow, reading his guidebook about the area, while Charlie and Lilly ventured inside.

The church was almost empty – the only other occupants were a couple of Japanese tourists with camcorders and a few parishioners, sitting silently in pews near the front. Charlie and Lilly strolled around the interior in respectful silence. Daylight shone through the stained glass, patterning the pillars with spatters of coloured light and illuminating multiple carvings of saints and devils, threatening each other across the aisles. Charlie stood on tiptoe and peered at one of the angels. Its face was rendered almost expressionless by the erosion of time, but he thought it looked a bit like Lilly.

"Wow. Everything here is so old," the boy said, gently touching the angel's smooth stone cheek.

"Not as old as me," Lilly answered quietly. Catching Charlie's worried look, she wrinkled her nose and gave him a devilish wink. "But I don't look it."

They wandered in and out of sweeping arches, gazing up through motes of sun-speckled dust to the majestic beamed roof high above. Lilly let her eyes drift and gave a sudden gasp. Charlie looked around. The girl was squinting through the sunlight at a small stone gargoyle leering out of the wall. Peazle wandered in the front door.

"It's called a Green Man." The pickpocket studied the carving with scholarly interest. "They're carvings of ancient pagan deities - you find them in very old churches - left over from the times when Christianity hadn't quite stamped out old superstitions and beliefs. Pictures of primitive gods and goddesses mainly."

"You really have studied a lot in the last couple of centuries, haven't you?" Charlie looked impressed.

"Actually, I read it in the guidebook."

"This isn't a carving of a man, green or otherwise." Lilly reached out and tapped the grimacing stone face, withdrawing her hand quickly as if she expected it to bite. "It's Morgana."

There was a creak of old oak as one of the worshippers at the front of the church slowly stood.

"Fashionably late, Lilly?" he drawled.

At the sound of his voice, the girl stiffened.

He was a big man, almost as tall as Shadowjack Henry and just as impressive. He wore a long black coat, expensively cut, over a black leather waistcoat with gold buttons. His thick red hair was pulled into a severe ponytail and he sported a waxed handlebar moustache the same bright colour.

"Nice waistcoat," Peazle said.

"He looks like a ginger Zorro," Charlie whispered.

"Who's Zorro?"

"Wait a minute." The boy frowned. "I recognise this guy!"

Lilly did too.

"Uallabh?" She took a faltering step back, hand rising to her mouth.

"In the flesh." The tall man stepped up onto the back of his seat and strode gracefully towards them, over the tops of the pews. His boots were as black and shiny as the rest of his outfit and silver tips on the heels gouged little chips from the wood as he walked. The other parishioners looked up in horror and tutted loudly but Uallabh did not even spare them a glance.

"Pay no attention," he said, hopping off the last bench and giving a small salute to Lilly. "After all, I helped build the place."

"You look good for a thousand years old."

"I've lost weight."

Uallabh's voice was slow and languid, as if the centuries had rounded his accent the way it had the stone around him. He looked and sounded more like a Wild West gunfighter than a Celtic warrior of old. He nodded his fiery head in the gargoyle's direction.

"Had that put it there to let you know I'd been around. If you ever came back, that was."

He smiled, but his lips were thin and bloodless and the warmth didn't reach his eyes. It looked uncannily like the sneer on Morgana's rocky face.

"You must hae a great deal of patience."

Uallabh turned sharply. Duncan stood in the doorway, sword in hand. Shadowjack Henry lurked behind him, his huge figure blacking out the sun.

"You can't pull out a weapon in a church!" Charlie gasped, horrified.

"Patience? Oh, I do indeed," the tall warrior replied calmly, paying no attention to the boy. He held up his hands to show he was unarmed. "But, to be honest, I haven't been around lately. Over the centuries, I've been to quite a few lands. Yes. Done quite a few things."

He lowered his hands and turned back to Lilly.

"But I come back every few decades… to check on the place."

"It's quite a coincidence that you turned up at the same time as us," Peazle said.

"Oh no. I guessed you were coming."

"How?"

"You'll see." The tall man smiled his narrow smile again and glanced around. The Japanese tourists were pointing camcorders in his direction. He glared at them until they turned away.

"Too many prying eyes here, Lilly." Uallabh hooked his arm through the girl's and led her towards the chapel doorway. "I've rented a cottage nearby."

He cast an unhurried eye over the rest of the party.

"Do you trust your entourage?"

"They're not my entourage. They're my friends."

"Ah," Uallabh said casually. "I have no friends myself."

Politely, he stepped back to allow Peazle and Charlie out of the Chapel before following them into the sun. He pointed in the direction of a smallholding, just visible through the trees, on the other side of the valley.

"They may come if you wish," he said to Lilly. "You go first."

"He's a bit tetchy, isn't he?" Charlie hissed as the party set off.

"Maybe he doesn't like women to be late," Peazle whispered back.

"Maybe he's oot of his wits." Duncan led the way, hand on his sword.

The forest grew thicker, the hiss of the river louder and fat flies buzzed around their heads, as the sunlight struggled to penetrate the canopy of leaves. The highlander glanced back. Uallabh was at the rear walking side by side with Lilly. She was trying to ask him questions, but he didn't seem to pay her much attention. Instead, his eyes darted from side to side, checking each tree and bush.

It occurred to the highlander that the tall warrior had never once turned his back towards any of their party. Duncan was wary by nature but Uallabh's caution seemed excessive.

The boy nodded to himself and tightened the grip on his sword hilt.

Uallabh was expecting trouble.

Inspector Archer rang the Wilson's doorbell and was answered by the sound of running feet. The front door jerked open and Charlie's father stood there, blinking. He looked as if he hadn't slept all night.

"Is my boy all right?" he said, naked fear in his eyes. "Have you heard anything?"

"I have tentative good news, Mr Wilson." Inspector Archer removed his hat and peered into the hall. "Is your wife around?"

"No. She's out searching the town for any sign of Charlie."

"Mr Wilson. Your son was captured on CCTV getting on a train for Edinburgh yesterday - apparently boarding of his own accord." The policeman hesitated. "He was accompanied by a boy wearing a bowler hat. You know any kids who wear something like that?"

"I don't keep up with children's fashion trends," Charlie's father replied witheringly. "And my son isn't the type to just take off."

"Do you know any reason why he would want to go to Edinburgh?"

Charlie's father shook his head.

"We took him there last year but he didn't seem to enjoy it much." He looked doubtful. "I... eh…"

"Anything at all would be helpful."

"He met a girl there that he seemed to like, except we don't know who she is. And he's seemed… I don't know… different since. More serious." Charlie's father smiled wanly. "I didn't think he *could* get more serious."

"So he might have secretly gone north to see this girl?"

"Not without telling me. It's not like I'd object if he wanted a girlfriend."

Inspector Archer shut his notebook without writing anything in it. He hadn't expected to learn anything new.

"Your son's details have been circulated to the Edinburgh police," he said gently. "All we can do now is wait."

Charlie's father put a hand on his arm.

"I don't know the Edinburgh police." His grip was tight, betraying the hidden strength all acrobats have. "But I think I know you. I've looked into your eyes and

I've seen a good man. A man who cares. I want you to lead the investigation."

"I'm with Birmingham CID, sir. The police up north know the terrain."

"Fine." Charlie's dad let his hand drop. "In that case, I'll go myself."

"I'd strongly advise against that." Inspector Archer began. But Charlie's father cut him off.

"I understand," he said. "And you understand that I can't take that advice."

It struck Archer that, behind the dishevelled appearance and meek manner, Charlie's father was as handsome as his wife was beautiful. And he was dealing with his grief and worry with a calm dignity that the Inspector rarely saw. He wondered what the boy was like. For the second time, he felt compelled to do something against his nature.

"Give me three days," he said suddenly. "It's the best I can do." He put the notebook in his pocket and shuffled awkwardly on the doorstep. "Mr Wilson. What do you make of this cat with hands business?"

Charlie's dad looked out across the suburban landscape.

"Him thought there was come into this land griffins and serpents," he quoted. "And him thought they burnt and slew all the people in the land."

"Pardon?"

"It's from *Le Morte d'Arthur* by Mallory. The point is, Inspector, it doesn't matter what kind of monsters are out there. All that matters is that we fight them."

The Inspector looked impressed.

"You're certainly a well-educated acrobat, Mr Wilson."

"Like you, I prefer action to words." Charlie's dad gave a grim smile. "That's why sitting doing nothing hurts so much."

Morgana

Uallabh's cottage was clean and simple, with old fashioned whitewashed walls and sturdy oak furniture. Curious about his new ally, Charlie glanced around, looking for the warrior's personal things - but there were no pictures on the walls and no mementoes on the dresser, window sill or table.

"I have enough memories," said the Uallabh, following the boy's gaze. "I don't need reminding of the things I've seen."

"Are you expecting trouble?" Duncan pointed to a profusion of bolts on the inside of the door. The highlander ran his hand over one, sniffed his fingers and wrinkled his nose. The locks were either new or had been oiled recently.

"I'm always expecting trouble," Uallabh muttered, sitting down on the only chair in the room – carefully positioned, Duncan noticed, so that it wasn't in a direct line of any of the windows. The rest of the Clan unfastened their rucksacks and flopped down on the polished wooden floor. They were getting used to rooms that didn't have enough seating for all of them.

"So, Lilly. I take it you have come for your father's cup?" From the casual way Uallabh asked, it was obvious he already knew the answer.

"Yes," Lilly nodded. "I got a little delayed."

She looked around. The rest of the Clan were watching them both intently.

"Eh… what exactly did happen all those years ago?" Peazle piped up. "If you don't mind us asking?"

"Aye," Shadowjack joined in. "Lilly told us how you ran from the Gorrodin-Rath…"

"I did not run," Uallabh interrupted. "I was ordered by Arthur to take the Grail to a place of safety."

He turned to Lilly.

"I wanted to return and help." The warrior lowered his head in shame. "But I swore an oath…"

"I understand," Lilly said, her eyes fixed on the ground. "Morgana put a curse on me. Took away my memory and made me blame my father for everything that had happened."

Uallabh raised an eyebrow. "But you remember now?"

"I knew nothing until yesterday." Lilly smiled gratefully at Peazle, who shrugged and went a little red. "In some ways, I wish I was still in the dark."

"And what happened to the monster?" Uallabh said brusquely. He had the same forthright manner as Duncan, or perhaps he did not want Lilly to dwell on her pain.

"A picture paints a thousand words." Lilly flexed her fingers and took a deep breath. "I'm not much of a sorcerer but I can do a few basic tricks." She held her tiny hands out and slowly opened her palms. A shimmering picture began to spread across the far wall, congealing into a sharp image like ripples settling on a pond. The others looked at it in amazement – all except Peazle, who had seen Jack Thane work the same spell.

The Clan found themselves looking at a battlefield. The constant hiss of the rain was mingled with the cries of the dying and the ring of metal upon metal. Strewn across the sodden moor were the bodies of perhaps fifty Gorrodin-Rath, the downpour washing blood from their misshapen white corpses. Round each monstrous carcass lay a dozen or more of Arthur's warriors, weapons still clenched in their lifeless fists. For the first time, Charlie understood just what a sacrifice these men had made in taking on Morgana's army. Yet, despite horrific casualties, they drove the Gorrodin-Rath towards the caves of what would eventually be named Arthur's Seat.

A hulking figure came tearing across the heather behind the unsuspecting men. The Clan flinched. As Lilly had stated, its face was a replica of the carving on Rosslyn Chapel wall.

"My mother," said the girl sadly.

Morgana ran with long jerking strides, straight for a group of warriors clustered around a fluttering pennant. It wasn't hard to guess who she was trying to reach.

Arthur and his men turned as Morgana reached them and the warriors clustered around their leader in a vain attempt to protect him. Morgana's windmilling claws ripped the defenders apart and she lunged at Arthur, just as the knight swung Excalibur at her. Morgana gave a shriek and staggered back, scrabbling at her side, inky gore spurting through her fingers. Arthur too stepped away, one hand clutching at his chest, blood seeping from a great gash just above the breastplate. With a look of surprise, he sank slowly to his knees and toppled over.

There was a sharp exhalation of breath from Uallabh's chair.

"My Lord," he said, his voice trembling. It was the first time the Clan had heard him show any real emotion.

Morgana retreated from the carnage, still trying to stifle the flow of blood. She turned and loped away, roaring to her own army as she retreated. But the Gorrodin-Rath had seen their leader attack the enemy rear and they rushed at Arthur's warriors with renewed fury. Charlie shuddered involuntarily. He spotted Mordred swinging a huge bloody club, leading the charge against his assailants. Surprised by the sudden advance, the humans fell back – thought they recovered quickly and launched themselves forward again with a determination that easily matched their foes.

"The sun is coming up!" Charlie pointed to the wall. The mountain tops behind the battlefield were beginning to glow with soft golden light.

The Gorrodin-Rath had spotted the sunrise too. With a furious roar, most turned and fled for the safety of the caves, while a few of the most loyal grouped around Morgana, begging her to save them.

The monster closed her eyes and spread both claws, muttering an incantation. A shimmering blue light appeared beside her and several creatures stumbled through. But the effort took all Morgana's power and the luminescence quickly faded again.

Abandoning the rest, Morgana turned and vanished over a hilltop, seeking Lilly and the cup.

"Where did Morgana go after she had dealt with you?" Charlie asked Lilly. "How did she remain hidden for hundreds of years?"

"I presume she had enough strength to open a thin place one more time," Lilly replied. "Go through it herself before she succumbed to her wounds."

"Jack Thane thinks she ended up in the land of Toth," Peazle said.

"Toth?"

"There are lands tae the west and north of Galhadria where nobody ever goes." Duncan counted off exotic names on his fingers. "Alabarra and The Wooded Kingdom in the north and west. Monshorn to the south and Toth in the east. I have never been there."

"There are impassable mountains separating Toth from Galhadria," Peazle confirmed. "A huge wall guards the only pass, but I was not allowed to see it."

"I wonder what brought Morgana back after all this time?" Uallabh's direct question showed his warrior instinct was keen as ever. None of them had an answer but Charlie noticed that Lilly gave a little glance in his direction. Everyone but Uallabh was aware he had killed the creature's son. It suddenly occurred to him how similar the two had looked and a horrible thought sprang into his mind.

"It's hard to tell the females of the Gorrodin-Rath from the males," he said.

"So?"

"What if some of those creatures escaping through the thin place were female?"

Peazle suddenly realized what the boy was getting at.

"If they were, the Gorrodin Rath may have been breeding for over a thousand years, hidden in some far off land." His face paled. "If that were so, how many of them might there be now?"

Duncan pulled his sword closer to him.

"Enough for a great army," he said slowly.

The Cup

Shadowjack Henry went to the window and looked out. Rosslyn Glen was lit by a late afternoon sun, filtering through the trees and setting the tops aflame with golden light. For a second, he remembered his old life on earth, working a forge in a valley, not unlike this one. He stroked his beard then turned to Uallabh, sitting in his chair, fingers interlaced casually over his chest.

"What's your story, warrior?" he asked.

Uallabh drew a deep breath through his nose and let it out again. When he spoke, his voice was neutral.

"I was entrusted with guarding the wizard's cup after we took it from the Gorrodin-Rath," he said. "I drank from it, as you know."

The others nodded.

"I can still die in battle but I'm no longer affected by the passage of time." The warrior gave a wry smile. "As much a curse as a blessing, let me tell you. But it was the first and last time I used the Grail - I had no desire to end up like the Gorrodin-Rath."

The others were in full agreement with that sentiment.

"I guessed Lilly would not make it to Rosslyn Glen, not after what I had seen."

Uallabh sat straight in the chair and tilted his head back, staring at the ceiling. The room was growing darker as the sun sank and he slowly blended into the shadows.

"I had nowhere to go. My Lord and my Clan were destroyed and all that was left was my solemn oath to them. I took a ship to France and travelled without purpose. But word had spread of the treasure I carried. No matter where I went, I was followed by those who sought that power. I killed many times and nearly died just as often. After a few hundred years, that can get a little tiring, even for a fighter."

For the first time, Duncan looked at Uallabh with sympathy. He, too, knew what it was like to travel strange lands and hold little hope in his heart.

"I tried and carry on the work my lord Arthur had started," the warrior continued. "I founded an order of knights - the Templars - recruiting only those famed for their virtue, piety and chivalry."

Peazle nudged Charlie and pointed at the *Guide to Scotland*. He gave the boy a quick told-you-so look. Uallabh uttered a snarl of derision.

"I was not Arthur," he said, finally. "My knights became corrupted by lust for the very thing they were supposed to guard."

"What happened?" Charlie said with a sinking feeling.

"They turned against me," the warrior replied calmly, as if he were discussing the weather. "So I destroyed them."

The party sat in silence, heads bowed.

"I did not mean to cause you such pain, Uallabh," Lilly said softly.

"In the 15th century, I returned to Rosslyn and established this Chapel," the man continued as if he had not heard. "I was going to hide the Grail here in case Lilly ever came back."

He gave the girl a wink that seemed ghoulishly at odds with his expressionless voice. "However, legends about me had spread and, of course, men came looking. Lawless knights. Bounty hunters. Desperate men. All seeking the power of the cup."

He uncrossed his legs and slowly stood.

"I travelled the world again, taking the Grail with me, wherever I went. To this day, there are secret societies on earth who know my identity and what I have. They still send men to search for me."

He stood beside Shadowjack Henry and looked with him out of the window.

"I kill them too."

Shadowjack put a hand on Uallabh's shoulder. The warrior did not seem to notice.

"But you knew to come back here, now? After all this time." Duncan could not keep the suspicion from his voice. "Just before we arrived?"

"A few months ago, I was living in Prague," Uallabh said. "I like it there. Lots of old buildings. But I can't stay too long in one place, for people grow suspicious when I don't age. That's why I can't have friends or a family."

Charlie saw Lilly's shoulders tighten. Talking about families was definitely a sore point with most of the Clan.

Uallabh walked across the room and opened an oak door. Beyond was a bedroom. The Clan could see a long black shape taking up half the floor. With a start, Charlie realised it was a coffin, its lid fastened with an enormous lock. Uallabh smiled grimly.

"I hide the cup in this when I travel. Customs officials are very keen to look in a trunk. Coffin's a different matter."

He fished about inside his waistcoat and pulled out a key on a leather thong around his neck. Watching the tall figure immaculately dressed in black, standing nonchalantly next to his coffin reminded Charlie of a picture he had once seen in a book.

A picture of Count Dracula.

He wondered how many other legends Uallabh had managed to start in his time on earth.

The warrior was now bending over the coffin and unlocking it.

"About six months ago, the Grail changed."

"Changed?"

"I didn't know what it meant," the warrior said. "But guessed it prudent to come back here... just in case,"

He lifted the creaking lid with no small effort.

The rest of the Clan trooped through to the bedroom and peered excitedly into the chest. Lilly was almost holding her breath.

The coffin was lined with white velvet. At the bottom was Gorrodin's wooden cup.

"It's been like that ever since," the warrior said.

Lilly stepped back, her mouth open.

For the Grail was softly glowing – gilded with beautiful, lambent flame.

The Eastern Wall

Jack Thane stood on top of the Eastern wall, staring into the pale grey morning. A brisk breeze ruffled his long dark hair and the goose feathers topping his boots. He put his hand on a shining silver rail and leaned out. The wall was so high that it was almost impossible to see its lower reaches, even if they had not been shrouded in morning mist. But he glimpsed the flash of a white hawk with black-tipped wings darting and swooping far below him.

No matter how many magical feats he might see, the wall never failed to impress him. It was as high as the sheer snow-topped peaks on either side - though the Lords' magic kept the curving structure free of ice. On either side, the craggy tops of the Fanfall Mountains stretched into the distance - an impassable natural barrier that separated the western edge of Galhadria from the desolate and forbidding land of Toth.

The wall stretched across what had once been a great pass - the only way through this impenetrable mountain range. At the base was an enormous barred gate that had once allowed travel between the two countries. It had rarely been opened in the last centuries

- for a long time dark creatures had prowled Toth and it was no longer safe for Galhadrians to enter.

Turning, Jack Thane stared back into his own land. Far below, he could see Castle Alclud – home of the Lords of the Western Wilderness - looking no bigger than a child's toy. Its myriad spires and minarets were slatted with shadows. It sat at the base of the Fanfalls and the morning sun had not risen high enough for its beams to dance across the walls and bring them to life. He let his eyes follow the path from the castle to the base of the wall, where a precarious staircase, cut from sheer stone, zigzagged up the surface.

He saw two small figures, fellow Lords, moving slowly up the steps, hundreds of feet below. Though they were too far away for him to make out their faces, he recognised both from their ways of walking. One was the leader, Tom Lincoln, the other Jenny Haa.

They could have flown up in an instant, but Jack Thane had recently insisted that the Lords of the Western Wilderness not use magic unless they had to. Their powers were immense, but their magic was not infinite. And Thane knew they would soon need all the sorcery they possessed to keep the enemy at bay.

Lords of the Western Wilderness. Jack Thane sorely disliked that title. As a young man, he had roamed the green hills of his world, coming and going as he pleased. He had been a master of the lyre and was often asked at villages he travelled through to host dances. He would strum into the night while maidens danced and men brought him cups of wine made from the finest fruit in their vineyards.

That was an age ago. Now he was stuck here, at the farthest corner of his domain, with only other sorcerers for company – protectors of their world. The Lords neither sang nor danced and they talked of nothing but pills and potions.

Tom Lincoln and Jenny Haa suddenly appeared at the top of the wall. They had tired of walking and had spirited themselves up the last half mile. Jack Thane frowned. If they knew how much magic they were going to need in the coming months, they would not use any on such trivialities. He bowed in reluctant greeting.

"You are early, Master Lincoln."

"I am," Tom Lincoln replied brusquely. "And I would like to know what is so urgent that you have called me to the top of this wretched place." He waved a dismissive hand in the direction of the mountains. "There is nothing to see here."

"If only that were true." Thane sighed theatrically, raising his eyes to where the sun was beginning to disperse the grey haze in the sky. "In truth, I'm afraid to even look down."

"I did not know you were fearful of heights," Tom Lincoln replied sarcastically. He was impatient to be back in Castle Alclud, where he had more important tasks to perform.

"If that were all I was scared of, I would still be asleep." Thane pointed over the edge of the wall.

"Look down into Toth again, Master Lincoln, for the morning mists are clearing."

Grunting sourly, the sorcerer bent his short, thin body and peered over the side of the wall. At first, he saw nothing. But, gradually, the haar dispersed and patches of the dull olive landscape of Toth started to show. He gave a gasp.

"There is movement!"

Jack Thane nodded. Jenny Haa pushed back her green hood and she too squinted over the parapet.

"It was the same yesterday," Thane said.

The last traces of mist had dissipated and Tom Lincoln's eyes widened as he took in the magnitude of what he saw. At the end of the pass was a mass of slowly moving white and grey, as if Toth were covered in a carpet of maggots. Though the distance made the creatures below smaller than insects, their numbers were vast. The sorcerer was looking at an army. Not simply hundreds, but thousands of monsters milling around.

"The Gorrodin-Rath." He whispered in horror.

"I had hoped this time would never come," Thane sighed. "Despite all my plans and preparations, I never really believed it would happen."

"But it is day!" Lincoln's face betrayed his puzzlement and anger. "They cannot come out in the day!" He struck the wall a furious blow with his fist and Jenny Haa flinched, stepping quickly back from the edge.

"You have eyes." Jack Thane was unmoved by this display of temper. "They have the power."

"They cannot!"

"Will you still not believe?" Thane cried angrily. "For months, I have been trying to convince the other Lords. I tell you, the Dolorous Stroke has been struck!"

Jenny Haa put a hand to her mouth.

"I do not know when or how," the sorcerer continued. "But it must have been done by one of our people - and against the Gorrodin-Rath. That is why their leader Morgana has awakened and her wounds have healed. That is why the Rath have grown so strong."

Tom Lincoln stood back from the wall. The evidence was right below him and he could not ignore it. Jack Thane was right and no amount of protesting would change that.

It was time to act.

"Have the Gorrodin-Rath tried to escape Toth by using Thin Places?"

"They have searched. But I sealed all those in Toth centuries ago."

"And the wall?"

"To reach us, they must overcome it. But it will take all our powers to keep it standing and the enemy will grow ever stronger. Eventually, we will not have the power to keep them at bay."

"I trust you have a plan, Master Thane? You have never been the patient sort."

"Of course." Jack Thane bowed meekly. "But it depends on a human pickpocket and his ragtag friends."

Jenny Haa looked fearfully over the wall again.

"I do not understand," she said. "If the Gorrodin-Rath are trapped in Toth, how could one of us strike a blow against them? Why *would* we?"

Jack Thane shot out a hand and grasped her arm. His face was set in a determined grimace.

"That is no longer important," he said, with quiet menace. "But we will *not* use any more magic until the Gorrodin Rath attack. Understood?"

He turned and stormed off down the staircase without looking back.

The Getaway

"Uallabh, I wish to free my father and return the Grail to him."

Duncan moved a little closer to Lilly as she made her announcement. Uallabh had killed everyone else who came looking for the cup and the highlander didn't want his friends to be next. Uallabh opened a cupboard door and removed a long black cloak from a plastic hanger.

"If I knew where your father was trapped, I'd have handed back his accursed cup centuries ago." He fastened the cloak around his neck and slipped his arms through short wide sleeves. Now he looked even more like a vampire.

"There is one small problem," Lilly said. "Morgana is back and is seeking the Grail to increase her power."

"As I said. Many have sought to take the cup from me. They have all failed."

"Nobody like Morgana."

"The only time I saw nobility in my fellow men was when Lord Arthur and his sorcerer Gorrodin were around to guide them." Uallabh pulled on a pair of black leather gloves. He drew himself erect and smoothed down his cloak. "You want to return the

Grail to your father? Tell me where he is and I'll be happy to take you."

"Take us?"

"Yeah. I've got a van outside." Uallabh pulled a set of keys from inside his cloak and jingled them. "How do you think I lug that coffin around? On a mule?"

"I'm not sure of the exact location where my father is trapped," Lilly sighed. "So much has changed over the centuries."

"How about a hint?"

"It was the northwest."

"That'll do me." Uallabh headed for the door. "We can work it out later when we're far from this place."

Night was falling when the Clan left the cottage. The woods were tall stripes of darkness and a thick cloud of floating insects attacked a bare electric light suspended above the back door. They had drawn lots and Charlie got the short straw. His rucksack now contained the Grail, carefully rolled inside a sleeping bag.

"That makes you prime target numero uno," Peazle smirked.

"I've got the power of immortality in this bag," Charlie said, awestruck. "I wonder what it would be like to live forever?"

Peazle looked at him with something akin to pity.

"Charlie. At the moment, you're the only one here who won't."

The boy stopped in his tracks. He hadn't thought of that.

"Immortality's not what it's cracked up to be," Uallabh led them down the crunching gravel path where a white transit slumbered at the end of the wooded drive. "Should I bring my coffin? You can sit on it in the back of the van."

"Thanks… but I'm used to the floor."

"It's bound to come in handy for something."

"No doubt," Shadowjack snorted. "We can use it if one of us dies."

There was an awkward silence. The big blacksmith grimaced at his own stupidity.

"I think we'll leave the coffin behind." Uallabh took out a flashlight as he reached the van, shone it carefully around the surrounding forest, then over the vehicle. Along the side in black lettering, the Clan could make out the words.

U. St Clair. Antiques.

"Everything looks safe."

"Nice touch," said Shadowjack, slapping the logo on the side. "Though I just made a wee bet with Peazle that it would say Exterminator."

He gave Uallabh a friendly smile. Uallabh sniffed and tried a half-hearted grin back, but only one side of his mouth curled up and it looked more like a sneer. He was evidently out of practice at being sociable.

"Sit with me, highlander," he said, handing Duncan the keys to the vehicle. "You look like a natural fighter and you never know what we might encounter. There's enough room for the rest of you in the back. I have one last errand to do in the house."

He trotted towards the cottage. Duncan looked at the keys and then at the passenger door. There was a little silver circle below the handle - that must be a lock. He tried two or three different keys until one fitted. He turned it and the door clicked open.

"Who says I cannae handle modern technology?" The highlander gave a thumbs up.

"Duncan?" Lilly interrupted the highlander's smug observations. "Turn and look at the woods. Do it slowly."

The highlander cautiously twisted his head.

A dozen pairs of glowing eyes stared at them from the blackness between the trees. Whatever was watching couldn't be more than fifteen yards away. Duncan inched round until he could see in the other direction. Shadowjack was standing near the back of the van, rucksacks scattered around his feet. Charlie and Peazle were hiding behind him, staring fearfully into the forest. Uallabh came out of the cottage, closed the back door and came striding towards them. His step faltered as he realised something was badly wrong. A glance at the forest stopped him dead.

One set of eyes blinked and moved forward, the creature behind it taking shape, as it emerged from the trees. It was a large dog, fur matted and dirty and cracked flesh showed through bare patches of mange. The hound's slavering mouth was drawn up over yellow fangs and white spittle dripped from its foaming muzzle. It emitted a low, trembling growl that made the hair stand up on Charlie's neck.

"Does it have a name tag?" Peazle said timidly.

"Not unless it reads Hound of Hell." Duncan looked longingly at his sword, still inside the fishing rod holder, next to the pile of rucksacks. Shadowjack took a tentative step towards the nearest canvas sheath - the one that held Excalibur. The dog growled again and tensed its hind legs. Other glittering eyes began to move closer and the Clan could make out the outline of several more large canines hidden among the trees.

"Don't move, Shadowjack," hissed Duncan urgently.

"I'm a statue."

"This is Morgana's doing," Lilly breathed.

"We're only going to get one chance," Uallabh's voice remained calm, despite the predicament. The dog swung its head towards him and gave a low snarl but didn't move any closer.

"Charlie, can you drive?"

"I'm twelve."

"In that case, wait until I give the word," the warrior continued. "I want you, Peazle, Lilly and Shadowjack to pull open the back doors of the van, jump inside, and close them as quick as you can." He turned his head in the highlander's direction, careful to keep the rest of his body motionless. "Duncan. You get in the front and unlock the driver's door for me."

"How do I do that?"

"What?"

"The only motor vehicle I've ever been in is an autobus. And that was four hours ago."

Uallabh let out a groan. The dog took another step forward and shook its head menacingly, white flecks curling around its neck like a shimmering collar. Duncan could see it was working itself up for an attack - and that might come at any second. He had no doubt the other canines, still lurking in the trees, would be quick to join in.

"Look in the passenger window," Uallabh said softly. "Do you see a square, grey catch on the driver's side?"

"I see it."

"You pull that."

"Got it."

"Now everybody, when I shout *go,* get yourselves into that van as if your life depended on it. Which it probably does."

Uallabh seemed to have a knack for finding humour in grisly situations.

Duncan was still peering in the passenger window, trying to adjust his eyes to the darkness inside. He tried to see into the back of the van but it was separated from the front by a curtained partition. He noticed the driver's window was rolled down a few inches and his eyes darted down to the driver's seat. It seemed to have some kind of dark covering. So did the passenger seat. And the dashboard.

They were covered in feathers.

The highlander pushed himself away from the car with a cry.

"Go!" roared Uallabh, startled by Duncan's sudden movement.

"Uallabh! Wait!"

The highlander was too late. Uallabh was already racing for the driver's side of the van. As he shot past, Shadowjack reached round, hauled open the van's back doors and Lilly sprang onto the runner board, ready to dive inside.

She got no further. A great inky mass surged from the interior of the van, enveloping her completely. With a strangled cry, the girl was catapulted backwards through the air, her head and torso completely hidden by a rustling, quivering black cloud. Peazle and Charlie threw themselves at the ground, but Shadowjack was caught in the surging wave, his top half obliterated by blackness.

"Crows!" he bellowed, swiping at the air, his voice muffled by hundreds of flapping wings. "They're attacking me!"

Lilly dropped out of the blackness like a stone and crashed to the ground as the flock of black crows swooped upward in a perfect arc. Shadowjack sank to his knees beside her, his beard bristling with feathers and his face covered in tiny lacerations. Uallabh skidded to a halt, looking confused.

The dog seized its chance and lurched forwards, bounding towards Lilly's unconscious body. Duncan ran for his sword. Peazle and Charlie pulled themselves to their feet and got between the girl and the slavering animal as the rest of the hounds burst from the woods. Each was wild and scabrous and every bit as big as their leader. Duncan appeared at Peazle's side, his own sword in one hand and Excalibur in the other.

There were four sharp cracks behind them and the lead dog and three others jerked sideways and crumpled into the ground. The others stopped in confusion, ears flat against their snarling skulls, stomachs pressed against the earth. Duncan whirled around.

Uallabh was clutching a smoking pistol in each hand.

"Swords were all very well in your day, highlander," he chuckled as the dogs reversed, snarling, back to the trees. "This is the 21st century."

The crows attacked again.

They came down at rocket speed, with a sudden rush of air and the deafening beating of wings. Seconds later, the Clan were enveloped in a whirling black mass. They tore frantically at the feathered air as claws and razored beaks raked their faces and hands, each jab drawing fresh blood. The dogs stopped retreating, turned, and crawled towards them again.

"The van!" Uallabh shouted. He fired several times up into the swirling cloud, then threw himself to the ground. "Crawl under the van!"

Charlie and Peazle dropped to their stomachs and wormed their way backwards, wriggling under the vehicle, dragging Lilly with them. The gravel ripped at their hands and knees, but the damage was nowhere as severe as the birds were causing, slicing at the back of their heads and battering them with their wings.

"I knew I shouldn't have packed my bowler hat away," Peazle cursed. "I need a helmet."

"I don't fit!" Shadowjack had tried to squeeze his massive body under the vehicle but he was too large to get more than the bottom half into the protected space. His arms were slapping at his exposed head, trying to stop the crows from reaching his eyes.

But the birds were now ignoring them and concentrating on the pile of rucksacks instead. They pecked and clawed at the fabric and several crows grasped the straps of Charlie's bag, flapping furiously as they tried to lift it off the ground.

"They're after the Grail!" Charlie shouted.

It was more than the boy could bear. He had abandoned his old life and his parents to get his hands on Gorrodin's cup. Lilly lay unconscious and bleeding beside him and he and his friends were trapped under a van by a bunch of birds, watching feral dogs closing in on them, like sharks circling a sinking ship.

"Sod this."

Charlie hauled himself out from under the van, put his head down and ran straight into the throng of frenzied birds. He grabbed the rucksack and hauled as hard as he could, popping the straps from the beaks of the screeching crows. The boy kept going, carried through the flock by sheer momentum. The birds rose behind him, a tattered black cloak, lined with beak and claw, ready to swoop back down and smother him.

There was only one place to head.

"No! Not the house!" he heard Uallabh shout. But it was too late. He hit the back door of the cottage and burst inside.

The birds turned and streamed after him, pouring through the open door, right behind the terrified boy. Shadowjack, Peazle and Duncan rolled out from the van, ready to go after their friend.

"Look at the woods!" Uallabh cried from under the van. A black-gloved hand stretched out from behind the back wheel, waving a gun in the direction of the forest.

Now there were over twenty pairs of eyes staring malevolently from the trees. The gloved hands pulled the trigger of one gun, then the other. The weapons clicked uselessly.

"I've run out of ammunition."

"Bet you wish you had a sword now," Duncan remarked scathingly.

The dogs attacked again.

The Coffin

Charlie tore through the living room, a split second ahead of the screeching black torrent and shot into the bedroom, slamming the door behind him. The wood shook and buckled as the combined weight of hundreds of crows slammed into it. The boy desperately looked around for something to wedge under the handle but the room was empty, except for the bed and the coffin.

"What kind of person only has one chair in his whole sodding house?" he wailed, as the door splintered and burst. With an acrobatic leap, The boy flung himself headlong into the coffin, reaching up and hauling the heavy lid down behind him - severing the wings and beaks of the leading birds, who were trying to struggle through the closing gap. Only one made it inside before the top slammed shut. In the pitch darkness, Charlie felt the furious creature worming its way up his body, trying to reach his face.

"One against one this time," he said with a grimace, grabbing the crow and wrenching at its neck until it snapped.

A noise like thunder reverberated through the claustrophobic blackness and the satin around him began to vibrate. Charlie covered his head with his hands.

The birds were attacking the coffin.

The pack of snarling dogs burst out of the woods and pelted towards Shadowjack, Duncan and Peazle. Peazle tossed one sword to the blacksmith and Excalibur to Duncan, who caught it gingerly and gave an experimental swing.

"Just like old times, eh?" Peazle had hauled one rucksack onto his back and was fastening another to his front.

"Padding," he explained.

Then the dogs were on them. Duncan and Shadowjack stood back to back, feet planted wide apart, and Peazle danced around between them, trying to stay out of the way of their swinging swords. The dogs raced around the party, leaping forwards, then jerking back, snapping at the air with slavering jaws, trying to get hold of the easiest target. Duncan was a fine swordsman and Shadowjack made up for his lack of expertise by sheer bulk - but Peazle had only the rucksacks for protection. The pickpocket desperately twisted and turned, trying to kick at snarling muzzles that drew closer with each rabid lunge.

"Uallabh!" Duncan took a swipe at one bounding dog and it skidded sideways with an agonised yelp. "What are you doing? We can't hold them off forever."

There was silence from under the van. Uallabh was nowhere to be seen.

"That sneaky bissom! He's abandoned us!" Duncan thrust angrily to the left and speared a slavering hound. As he twisted the blade to free it, another dog leapt onto his exposed back, fangs inches away from his face. Shadowjack elbowed it into the air and the hound snapped at Peazle as it landed, almost taking off his hand.

The pickpocket was near to crying. A large greyhound leapt past him, fastened itself to Shadowjack's side and bit deep into his flesh. With a roar, the blacksmith brought a meaty fist crashing down on its head. The dog went rigid and dropped away.

There was a rapid succession of shots from somewhere behind. Three of the hounds span away from the attack and collapsed, writhing on the ground. Duncan risked a glance in the direction of the shooting. Uallabh was standing by the cottage, fumbling in his pocket.

The dogs peeled away and headed for him before he could find more bullets and reload again. Instead of ammunition, however, the warrior pulled a small square object from his pocket. It was a sturdy Zippo lighter and Uallabh flicked it to life with a practised roll of his thumb. With a jerk of his gloved hand, he broke a pane of the window and tossed the lighter through.

The dogs were now only feet away, their legs a blur of motion. As the leading hound leapt for his throat, Uallabh threw himself to the side, rolling twice and then scrabbling behind a stack of logs.

The house exploded.

Huge yellow fireballs billowed out of every window. The dogs were engulfed in mid-stride - half the pack wiped out instantly in the flaming inferno. Even Shadowjack was knocked flat by the force of the blast, bowling over Duncan and Peazle as he fell. Ash and burning feathers floated all around them, coating the white van and settling on the blackened corpses of the charred hounds. The few survivors broke off their attack and slunk back into the woods, howling mournfully as they went.

Ears ringing, Peazle lifted his head from the gravel and stared in disbelief at the cottage - or what was left of it. The explosion had blown out the windows and destroyed the masonry surrounding them. The front door was a warped, smoking lump lying yards away from its blackened frame. The strength of the blast had been so great, it had extinguished the flames instantly, but the entire building was reduced to a charred hollow. Nothing inside could have survived.

"Aw, Charlie," Peazle moaned, burying his face in his hands. The pickpocket had dragged the unwilling boy on this adventure and had got his friend killed. A clogging wad of regret rose in Peazle's chest and he burst into tears.

Uallabh, face blackened by ash and dirt, pulled himself up from behind the log pile.

"What have you done?" Duncan rose unsteadily, swaying from side to side, sword clutched menacingly in his hand.

"I turned on a gas canister when I left the house. First rule of staying hidden is leaving no evidence."

The warrior stumbled over the smoking ground to the broken remains of the bedroom wall and peered into the murky gloom.

"I left a candle burning. By the time the gas reached the flame, we should have been well on our way." He wiped his forehead with the back of his hand, leaving a sooty stripe. "The birds must have blown it out with their wings. Had to finish things off myself."

"You killed Charlie!" Shadowjack and Peazle were on their feet and Duncan looked ready to turn his sword on the warrior. Uallabh squinted through the smoke into the ruined bedroom. He seemed gruesomely calm.

"You know, they don't make coffins now like they used to," he said conversationally. "Had mine for 200 years - specially made. Lead lined, it is."

He pointed nonchalantly into the shattered room.

"Could even withstand an explosion."

The rest looked into the smouldering bedroom. In the centre of the charred floor lay the coffin, still intact. As they watched, the lid slowly creaked open and Charlie sat up, holding his rucksack. He looked around at the devastation, blinking.

"I like what you've done with the place," he said. "Not a bird in sight."

Uallabh's van hurtled through the night, keeping to the smallest, most secluded roads, always heading north. Peazle sat in the front seat beside the warrior, a map of Scotland on his knees.

The rest of the Clan were in the back. Lilly was finally awake, lying with a wet towel pressed to her head. Apart from that, she was virtually unscathed, having spent the entire battle out cold under the van. The rest looked like death warmed up, their clothes covered in grime and their faces and hands lacerated by beaks and teeth. Uallabh had tied a bandage around Shadowjack's bloody midriff - a task that had emptied the van's medical kit of gauze. Fortunately, the wound was not deep enough to be serious.

"We'll stop and rest somewhere when we get further away," the warrior shouted back. "We can't be too careful - as you now probably agree."

"Can we clean the van out when we do?" Charlie poked around the floor with his foot. "All these feathers are bothering my asthma."

"I can't believe you booby-trapped your own house," Peazle said to Uallabh, not without admiration.

"Standard practice."

"I can't believe I couldn't fit under the van," Shadowjack growled. "I'm definitely going on a diet."

The rest roared with laughter. Even Uallabh beeped his horn in appreciation. Only Duncan seemed solemn.

He crouched beside Lilly and helped press the towel against her broken skin.

"We barely survived that," he whispered. "And why were we attacked by animals?"

"Morgana must have been directing them from Toth. Some animals are easy to control - especially lower creatures like worms or starving, confused ones like stray dogs." Lilly felt the lump on her head and winced. "Carrion birds have always done the bidding of the darker forces - but usually as spies and thieves, not fighters."

"Either way, it means Morgana knows where we are."

"She'll always have some idea, as long as there are crows in the sky," Lilly conceded. "Every time we do something predictable, or stay in one place too long, she'll scrape together whatever she can control and assault us with them."

"At least she's not close enough tae fight us herself," Duncan said, always thinking of tactics.

"Thank goodness for that." The girl winced at the thought of battling her mother again. Then she frowned.

"Do you know how much power it must take to mount attacks like these from the other side of a Thin Place?"

Duncan didn't.

"The Lords of the Western Wilderness themselves couldn't do it." Lilly took the cloth from her head and dabbed at some of the blood on Duncan's face. She leaned close as she did so, so the others wouldn't hear.

"My mother never had power like that before, Duncan. Not even with the Grail."

"So what has happened?"

"I don't know." Her voice dropped even lower. "But if she gets her hands on the cup now, her abilities will be Godlike."

Duncan smiled grimly. "Then we'll have tae make sure she doesnae."

There was more laughter from the other occupants. Charlie had found some crisps and was refusing to give Shadowjack any, despite his pleas. Lilly pressed her knuckles against the side of her head and closed her eyes. Duncan wasn't sure if she was concentrating or just in pain. He sat back and rested his head against the metal skin of the van. The vehicle's movement made his teeth chatter and he gritted them together until his jaws ached.

He was deeply troubled. For a start, he did not trust Uallabh. During the fight at the cottage, the warrior had glanced in the bedroom window before he blew the house up - but how could he have been sure Charlie was safe in the coffin? Duncan had the horrible suspicion Uallabh had merely been trying to save his own skin.

And he was beginning to realise how formidable an adversary Morgana was. She was obviously clever and there was every chance she would guess where they were heading.

If she did, Duncan had no doubt there would be another ambush waiting for them when they got there.

Archer's Holiday Plan

Superintendent Lipton's office was painted battle-ship grey and smelled of cigarette smoke. It was like sitting in a giant ashtray, Inspector Archer thought. Across the dingy walls were splattered photocopies of wanted men and missing children, an arcade of black and white faces who had gotten lost one way or another. A large water cooler burped rudely in the corner.

"You've put in for a week's holiday, eh?" The superintendent scratched his yellow-tinged moustache and glowered at the Inspector's timesheet.

"I'm owed three."

"Where were you thinking of going? Venice? The pyramids? Butlins?" The superintendent tried to sound jovial, but Inspector Archer could sense a policeman's mind at work behind the seemingly innocent question. He decided to tell his boss the truth.

"I thought about going to Edinburgh. Heard it's pretty up there."

"Going on your own?"

"Who would I take?"

The superintendent picked up a small folder and flicked through it.

"This case you were working on. Charlie Wilson. Missing, eh?" He read quickly. "The boy was spotted taking a train to Edinburgh, along with another kid wearing...." he frowned over the top of the file. "A bowler hat. It's all very Oliver Twist."

Inspector Archer didn't reply.

"It's been reported to the authorities up north, Archer," the superintendent carried on. "Well out of your jurisdiction, I'd say."

Inspector Archer held his superior's stare.

"I'm going on holiday. That's all."

"Still... I'm sure you intend to drop in on the local police in Edinburgh. Just to keep your hand in." The superintendent's moustache bristled. It could have been a small smile or just a disapproving tightening of his lips.

"I might. Professional courtesy, after all."

"You've handled plenty of missing person cases. What's so different about this one?"

"I don't know." Archer let his eyes drop. "Just a hunch, sir, that's all."

The Inspector dropped the file back onto the desk.

"It's your holiday. You earned it. Do what you like."

"Thank you." Inspector Archer stood and made for the door.

"Inspector."

"Yes, sir?"

"Policing is about facts and hard evidence. Hunches don't work in the real world."

"I know, sir."

"Enjoy your vacation."

"I'll try."

Archer went out and closed the door. Superintendent Lipton sighed and shook his head, put away the file and lit a cigarette.

Charlie woke with a strangled gasp. His arms were pinned to his sides, and the air around him was bright and red - for a second, he thought he was back in Uallabh's coffin, surrounded by the flaming fireball that had destroyed the warrior's house.

Then he realised he was wrapped in a sleeping bag and daylight was glowing through the canvas sides of his tent. He struggled free of the bag and stuck his head out of the flap. The morning sun was moving through the trees, cutting bright swathes across a misty clearing. The rest of the Clan were sitting around a small fire, sipping coffee from tin mugs. Uallabh's van was parked at the edge of a rutted track that petered out where the clearing began.

"What time do you call this to be waking?" Peazle shouted cheerfully.

"The later I get up, the less of the day there is to get chased around by God knows what," Charlie replied sourly, climbing out of the tent and accepting a steaming mug.

"What's for breakfast?" he grunted, rubbing his eyes. "Berries and grubs?"

"There's still some prawn cocktail crisps." Shadowjack held out a crumpled packet. "I brought about twenty bags at a service station. I've become quite partial to them."

"We're trying to work out exactly where we're going." Duncan looked up. He, Uallabh and Lilly were bent over a map of Scotland, laid flat on the dewy grass and held down by rocks.

He turned to Lilly

"Describe where you lived with your father."

Lilly was staring intently at the map as if it were a jigsaw puzzle she didn't know how to complete.

"In the northwest highlands somewhere, beside a huge waterfall. He's in a cave nearby." She scanned the chart from coast to coast. "But there were no maps in those days - and the names of places have changed over the centuries. There are dozens of waterfalls marked here. I can't tell which one it is."

"Was there anything unusual about it?"

"Yes. My father picked it because there was a Thin Place nearby."

Charlie glanced at the chart. "I don't think *The Collins Touring Map of Scotland* lists those as a method of getting around."

"You're not really a morning person, are you Charlie?" Peazle rummaged in a bright blue rucksack. With a happy sigh, he pulled out his prized bowler hat and doffed it at them.

"I thought you threw that blasted thing away."

"Good job I didn't." Reaching inside the brim, the pickpocket pulled out a crinkled piece of parchment and tossed it to Uallabh. The warrior unfolded it and laid it on the grass. It was another map of Scotland, but this one had no roads or towns or any names at all. Instead, dotted over the surface were strange blue or gold spirals.

"A faerie map," Uallabh said, with a tinge of awe in his voice. "I've heard of them. Never actually thought I'd see one."

"I got it from Jack Thane," said the pickpocket proudly. "See those little swirls? Those are Thin Places - the blue spirals are the ones that can still be used. There are very few left and they're almost all in the far north. Probably because there are fewer people there."

The Clan gathered excitedly around the maps and compared them.

"Only one big waterfall has a Thin Place anywhere near it - and an open one too! Here, near the northwest coast. On the modern map, it's called Eas a Chual Aluinn Falls. - the highest waterfall in Britain."

"It's pretty remote."

"It's pretty hard to pronounce," Charlie scowled. "The nearest waterfall to my house is called Tumbley Dell."

Peazle circled the point on the map with a black pen. "Whatever it's called, that's where we're heading."

"Perhaps not." It was Uallabh who spoke and the rest of them looked at him in surprise. The warrior was studying the modern map carefully.

"Morgana can't know for certain where we're going," he said. "But she's bound to guess that Gorrodin's prison might be on the list."

Duncan nodded. He had already come to that conclusion himself.

"She knows what our van looks like and the northwest of Scotland is pretty desolate country. Great for a trap, if we're caught on some isolated country road."

"Then what do you suggest?"

"I suggest we fool her."

The War Council

Uallabh leaned forward and tapped the faerie map.

"Like Peazle said, there are very few Thin Places left open - but there is a cluster of them here in the far northeast. Up near this little town of Wick." He shifted his attention to the modern map. "And lo and behold, there's a rail line not far from here that runs north and ends at Wick."

"But the rail line runs up the *east* coast," Lilly protested. "We want to be heading for the west."

"I know. So what would Morgana think if we took that train? What would the Galhadrians think, for that matter? Don't forget, they must be wondering how we're getting on."

"They'd think we still intended to take the Grail to Galhadria - through one of the Thin Places!"

"Exactly. So let's board that train. Suppose Morgana has an ambush waiting at Eas a Chual Aluinn Falls. If her spies report we're heading northeast instead, she'll have to change plans - move her forces to stop us reaching the Thin Places there. That should even the odds a little."

"I can see where you're going with this," Duncan said approvingly.

"I can't," Shadowjack mumbled through a mouthful of crisps

"The rail line hugs the east coast for most of the journey but, right here, it veers inland to avoid crossing the Dornoch Firth." The warrior traced the route with a calloused finger, round a wide estuary jutting into the Scottish mainland. "The farthest point it moves inland is this wee station here, Lairg. No more than a village."

Peazle tapped the rim of the bowler hat thoughtfully against his lips.

"Lairg is about the same latitude as Eas a Chual Aluinn Falls."

"Exactly. So, what if one of us sneaked off the train there, carrying the Grail? Headed west on foot? It can't be more than 40 miles to the Falls, as the crow flies."

"Try not to use that expression."

"Sorry."

"I know that area," Duncan broke in. "It's not too far from the lands of my childhood."

In his head he was picturing precipices and glens more accurately than any map could portray them. He closed his eyes and made some mental calculations. "I could make it in a day and night's hard march."

"Meanwhile, the rest of us leave the train at Wick and try to keep out of Morgana's way. By the time her spies notice that Duncan is missing, he may well have reached Gorrodin and freed him. Then Gorrodin uses the Grail to rescue us."

Uallabh sat back and sipped his coffee.

"It's risky, I admit."

"Risky isn't the word for this plan." Shadowjack scratched his beard. "It's more…."

"Suicidal?"

"Insane?"

"Doomed?"

Everybody looked at the maps, willing them to somehow produce an alternative.

"I havnae got a better plan," Duncan sighed. "Does anyone else?"

Nobody did.

"Then let's break camp and get moving." Uallabh was already on his feet and dousing the fire. "You never know who might be watching."

Charlie and Duncan took down the tents. Lilly folded up the faerie map and Peazle tore off the section of the touring book that contained Eas a Chual Aluinn Falls and stuck it in the inside rim of his hat. Shadowjack began cleaning out the mugs with ash from the dead fire.

"A day and night staying ahead of Morgana," he said to Charlie, with a note of concern. "When we get to Wick, we better stock up on crisps. What flavour is your fav…." His voice suddenly trailed off.

A large crow was watching him from the long grass a few feet away.

"Charlie," he whispered. "That black beastie's been listening."

He lunged forward with surprising swiftness for a man so large. But the crow was already airborne, wings fluttering like black cloth. It deftly avoided Shadowjack's outstretched arms and rose steeply into the sky with a victorious caw, growing smaller with each beat of its wings.

A blur swept up over the top of the nearest tree and collided with the vanishing black shape. As the astonished Clan looked on, the crow spun sideways, trailing an arc of blood, then dropped like a stone. It landed with a thud on top of Uallabh's van.

A white hawk with black-tipped wings floating serenely in the air where the crow had been. It banked in a long leisurely turn and then hovered again, watching the Clan. Charlie looked vainly around for a rock to throw - he was sick and tired of being spied on by stupid birds - no matter who they reported to.

He heard a sharp crack to his right. The hawk remained motionless in the air for a second, then its wings folded and it fell from the sky, crashing to the ground a few feet from the campfire.

Uallabh lowered his pistol and tucked it back inside his coat.

"Like I say. You never know who might be watching."

He picked up his pack and lugged it to the back of the vehicle.

"I washed this van yesterday," he grumped, sweeping the crow off the hood with a contemptuous swipe.

The rest silently finished stowing the tents and picked up their remaining possessions. Uallabh beckoned to Duncan and the highlander climbed into the passenger seat beside the warrior. Peazle walked over and looked down at the dead hawk. The once-proud bird lay in the wet grass, a lump of bloody feathers.

"I told you, Jack Thane," he muttered to himself. "We have a different kind of magic here."

He stuck his bowler hat on his head and climbed into the back of the van.

The Lords of the Western Wilderness sat at a round table in the Whale Room. Jack Thane, Tom Lincoln and Jenny Haa were there. So were the other Lords - Prestor John, Gideon, Will Thorn, Mabon, Math and Baubi Ross. All waited in nervous silence until Lincoln raised a hand to formally begin their meeting.

"We are in grave danger, my friends." The old man's voice was quiet and strain had deepened the wrinkles on his face. "The unthinkable seems to have happened. The Dolorous Stroke has been struck - against the Gorrodin-Rath."

There was a muted gasp from the other wizards. Will Thorn rose, face red with anger. He was the youngest of the Lords and his dark, darting eyes were as quick as his temper.

"Who could have struck such a blow but one of us?" There was a murmur of agreement from some, while others shouted their own questions.

"When was this deed done?"

"How do we know this for sure?"

"ENOUGH!" Tom Lincoln bellowed and the outcry died down. "There will be time enough for recriminations if we survive. In the meantime, we must use every scrap of our powers to keep the Western Wall strong and the Rath contained."

He looked across at Jack Thane.

"One of us has already taken it upon himself to put an…operation into effect," he said bitterly. "It may afford us some small reprieve. You have the floor, Master Thane."

Jack Thane stood and gave a business-like bow.

"The Dolorous Stroke was designed to destroy the side that struck it." Despite this gloomy prognosis, the sorcerer seemed remarkably confident. "I, for one, am not going down without a fight."

Will Thorn and Prestor John nodded and the others muttered in agreement.

"The Stroke has awakened Morgana, leader of the Rath, and bestowed on her immense authority," Thane continued. "She hopes to increase that advantage even more by regaining Gorrodin's Grail."

There was an icy silence from the rest of the table. Gorrodin's name was never mentioned among them. Jack Thane paid no attention to their discomfort.

"Even without the Grail, she will triumph over us. But if she regains the cup, source of her original power, her victory will be swift and complete. Therefore, I have sent a party of humans to keep it from her."

The rest of the sorcerers were leaning forwards, eyes narrowed, listening intently.

"They have already located Gorrodin's daughter - the only link to the cup - and are trying to bring her back to safety. I am not sure of their present location, but I presume they are heading for a cluster of thin places to the north."

"You presume?"

"The hawk following them has not reported back," Thane said. "A victim of Morgana's forces, I imagine."

"What do you actually know?" Lincoln snapped

"They have been joined by Uallabh, one of Arthur's original knights." The wizard hesitated, then plunged on. "It is possible they may even have the Grail itself."

"I cannot believe you would entrust the fate of Galhadria to a bunch of humans!" Gideon now stood, hands wide, entreating his companions. "We should send one of our own to find and escort them back to Galhadria."

"None of us can leave anymore." Baubi Ross spoke quietly. "From now on, it will take the power of our combined talismans to keep the Rath at bay. We can no longer interfere, even if we want to."

Jack Thane permitted himself a superior smile.

"We must trust that the humans will thwart Morgana while I try to find a way to snatch victory from our sure defeat. As a young friend of mine once said, they have a different kind of magic."

Nobody at the table smiled.

"It does not matter." Mabon scolded. "If the Dolorous stroke was used by a Galhadrian against the Gorrodin Rath, they are destined to win. It's as simple as that."

"Grail or no Grail, I have a plan," Thane insisted. "I cannot divulge the details right now...."

"Why not?" Will Thorn objected. "Is this a play for power? How do we know it was not you who instigated the Stroke?"

"Or you!" Thane was quick to turn the accusation to his advantage. "It could have been any of us. In which case, I prefer to play my cards close to my chest."

"None of *us* are traitors." Thorn stammered.

"What of the Wilson child?" Math broke in. "He used Excalibur to kill Mordred. Could that not be the Dolorous Stoke?"

"Excalibur may be magical, yet it is simply a tool." Gideon shook his head. "The boy is a mere human. It was not him."

"If any of you have another strategy, I'd be happy to hear it," Thane snapped. "If not, let me try and save us in my own way."

The rest lapsed into sullen silence.

"Enough squabbling." Tom Lincoln brought proceedings to a close. "I agree the humans most likely move is to head northeast, to reach the thin places there. We will send what meagre forces we can muster to guard those and assist in their safe passage to Galhadria. This meeting is adjourned."

He banged a gavel sharply on the table and the sound rang ominously through the Whale Room.

"In the meantime, let us prepare for war."

END

Book Two of the Galhadria Trilogy

ABOUT THE AUTHOR

Jan-Andrew Henderson (J.A. Henderson) is the author of 31 children's, teen, YA, adult and non-fiction books. Published in the UK, USA, Australia, Canada, Germany and the Czech Republic, he has been shortlisted for thirteen literary awards and is the winner of the Doncaster Book Prize and the Royal Mail Award.

Subscribe to his website for regular free books, stories, news and advice

www.janandrewhenderson.com